Finding Pride

~ The Pride Series ~
Megan & Todd

Follow Jill online at:
Jill@JillSanders.com
http://JillSanders.com
Jill on Twitter
Jill on Facebook
Sign up for Jill's Newsletter

Dedication

This book is dedicated to the woman who read me my first book. In loving memory of a great woman and teacher…Thank you, Mom.

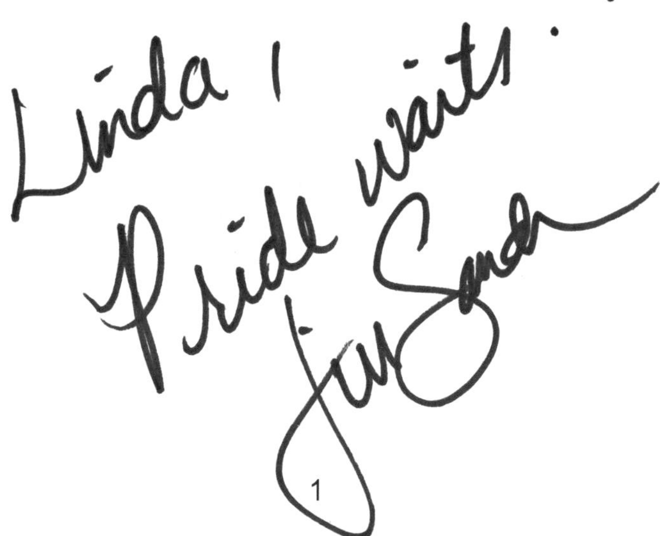

Summary

Megan Kimble has finally freed herself from years of abuse at the hands of her ex. Now she can finally start a new life and figure out just who she really is. When her brother Matt dies suddenly, she takes a big risk and moves cross-country to live in his house and take over his new business. This could be the chance she needs. There's only one problem now. She can't seem to escape the irresistible charm of her departed brother's best friend.

Todd Jordan just lost his best friend and business partner. When Matt's sister moves into town, his attraction to her is instant. Can he prove to her that all men are not the same and resist his own desires as she learns to trust again? Overcoming the odds is just part of their journey. The two must first survive a fateful visit from Megan's ex to have any chance at happiness.

Table of Contents

Finding Pride

Jill Sanders

Chapter One

As the sun disappeared behind a dark cloud, a white sedan crept slowly down the winding road. A wall of trees on either side gave the impression that the only way out was to forge ahead. The black pavement weaved around tight bends, up and down rolling hills. If you could witness the scene from above, it would appear similar to a white mouse running through a maze on its way to find some cheese.

Several minutes had passed since the last open field. Every now and then a quick glance of a farmhouse or a barn would appear. But for now, the only view was the gray of the sky, the green of the trees, and the dark surface of the road.

The car was traveling towards freedom that had come at the worst price: death. Megan Kimble had just lost the last of her family.

Hours later, the sun peeked out of the clouds, landing on the small crowd gathered around a casket. Mist and fog hung in the afternoon air. The sun's rays made the hill overlooking the small town of Pride, Oregon, appear to be cut off from civilization, like an island floating in a sea of fog. Not a sound came from the gathered mourners. Each person stood with their head down, looking at the dark, wet wood of the casket.

Megan stood in front of the crowd dressed in a dark skirt and a black raincoat. She looked down as tears silently rolled down her cheeks. Her long blonde hair was neatly tied back with a clip. The right sleeve of her coat hung empty, and her arm was tucked close to her body, encased in a white cast from her upper arm to just above her wrist.

Looking up, she gazed around the cemetery, not really noticing the people, only the old and crumbled headstones. Her eyes paused on a tall figure in the distance that appeared to hover above the mist. Blinking a few times to clear the moisture from her eyes, she realized it was a huge headstone in the shape of an angel with arms outstretched towards the heavens. It seemed to be reaching up in desperation, in need of a helping hand to ascend above.

Her thoughts drifted to Matt, and she looked back down at the casket. He had always called her his little angel. Looking at the simple wooden casket through teary eyes, she remembered her brother's face as it looked fifteen years ago when she had awakened in a hospital bed with her young body covered in bruises, the memories of violence by her father's hand gone, along with their parents' lives.

Matt's was the first face she had seen in the cold sterile room. His face had been streaked with tears, his eyes red as he'd comforted her. "Little Meg, everything will be okay. I'll take care of you now. Don't worry my little angel."

Her thoughts snapped back to the cemetery as they lowered the casket into the wet ground. What had she ever done to deserve such a great brother? What had she ever given back to him? He'd given up everything for her, yet she couldn't think of one thing she'd given him except lies.

Feeling hopeless and isolated, she began to wonder what she had left to live for. Why continue? She was all alone now; there was no one left to share her life with. Realizing it was probably Derek's influence causing her dark thoughts, she tensed. Lifting her head, she tried to dismiss the thoughts of her ex-husband. He didn't matter anymore, she told herself. He was out of her life forever.

As she stood in the old cemetery surrounded by a hundred strangers, she felt utterly alone. Matt had been her family, the only family that had really mattered. She had an aunt somewhere, but she hadn't seen or heard from the woman in over fifteen years.

Glancing over, she noticed the priest walking towards her and quickly wiped the tears from her face. He was a short, stout man who was dressed in long, black robes. He wore a wide-brimmed hat that covered his curly silver hair. His face seemed gentle and kind. She could see that his eyes were red from his own tears. He had been very generous in the words he'd spoken about her brother during the short service.

She wasn't Catholic. Neither was her brother, but at this point she wasn't going to object. It had been a wonderful service and so many people had turned out. She didn't know who had organized the service, but she was sure that the priest had had a big hand in it.

"Hello, dear, I'm Father Michael. We spoke on the phone a few days ago," he said, as he took her by the hand. His hands were warm and comforting. "Matt was such a nice young man. I'll miss him dearly."

"Thank you. I'm sorry I wasn't able to get here sooner. I would have helped you plan his service—"

"Don't mention it. We all pitched in to help. That's the wonderful thing about small towns." He smiled and patted her hand a little. "The people in Pride don't usually take to strangers, but Matt just fit in. He became part of the family, you might say. I know he wasn't Catholic, but he did enjoy a good sermon and always attended our social events. Your brother was very well liked around here."

It didn't sound like he was talking about her brother. Matt had always been somewhat of a loner and had never really taken to crowds. But then again, they'd grown apart from each other when he'd moved out west to Oregon.

As the priest continued talking to her about Matt and the town of Pride, she looked around at the crowd of strangers in the muddy cemetery. It appeared that the whole town had braved the wet weather for her brother's funeral. There were numerous faces, both young and old, many weatherworn from years on local fishing boats. She was used to being in crowds, having lived in a large city most of her life, but now it felt like every set of eyes were on her.

Shaking her head clear and taking another look around, she could see that, in fact, almost no one was looking directly at her. As her eyes scanned around, something else caught her gaze. A pair of the lightest silver-blue eyes she'd ever seen looked back at her through the crowd. The man stood a head taller than everyone else around him, and he was staring directly at her. For a moment, she forgot everything, including blinking.

The man had dark brown wavy hair, which was a little long and reached over his coat collar. From what she could see of him under his leather coat, he appeared to be thin. His face could have easily been etched in marble and put on display. His jaw was strong with the smallest of clefts in his chin. His lips were full and his nose was straight, but it was his eyes that caught her attention again. He was staring at her like he wanted to say something to her from across the crowded cemetery.

When Father Michael stepped between them, he broke the trance she'd been in. Blinking, she tried to refocus on the short priest. He was attempting to encourage her to stop by the church for services sometime.

"Megan, I feel like you're already part of the flock. I'm sure we'll be seeing you next week. If there is anything we can do for you, just let me know," the father said while patting her hand. "You will let us know if you need any help moving in, what with your hurt arm and all."

She looked down at her right arm enclosed in the white cast. She had it tucked closely under her raincoat, which she had left unzipped. The pain was a dull throb now, but that didn't make the terrible memories go away.

“The Jordans are your nearest neighbors. They were very good friends of Matt’s. The two boys are young and strong. I’m sure they’ll be glad to come down and help you move in your things.” There was a matchmaking look in the man’s eyes, and she tried to take a step backwards, but her hand was still engulfed by his larger one. “And I’m sure their sister is looking forward to getting them out of her hair for a few hours,” he said with a wink.

“Thank you, Father. I’ll try to stop by the church for services. I don’t have much to move in, only a few bags, but thank you for offering.” It was the truth. Megan had sold what little furniture she had left. In fact, she’d been living out of her suitcase for the past few weeks.

“Well, now, if you change your mind, let me know,” he said, patting her hand one more time.

Just then a large woman walked up to them. She had on a very bright blue dress covered in white flowers. Over it, she had a slick black raincoat that covered only half of the dress and half of the woman. She reminded Megan of a peacock all dressed up with its feathers ruffled.

“Father Michael, you let go of that girl’s hand so I can shake it. It’s a great pleasure to finally meet you, Megan,” the woman said while shaking her hand with a firm, warm grip. “I’m Patty O’Neil. I run the local grocery store. I’ve heard lots about you from your dear departed brother, God bless him.”

The woman quickly crossed herself and continued. "I'm sure proud to finally meet you. O'Neil's Grocery. It's right down on Main Street. You can't miss it," she said. "It's been in my family for generations. Well, if there is anything we can do…" She trailed off as the next person approached her.

And so it went, the entire town shaking her hand and offering their help in any manner possible.

Todd Jordan silently watched Matt's younger sister. He'd recognized her instantly from the picture Matt had kept on his desk. She was a lot thinner now and very pale. She looked lost. Her broken arm, which she held against her tiny body, made her look even more so. He'd scanned her from head to toe when she'd arrived at the cemetery. The raincoat she wore reached halfway down her slender body, and her heels looked very sensible as they sat halfway sunk in the mud.

He remembered Matt telling him that she was recently divorced but couldn't remember any more details. All he knew was that his friend hadn't been happy about the circumstances. His thoughts were interrupted when Father Michael approached him.

"Well, now, young Todd." The father always called him "young" even though he was now in his mid-thirties. "It's a shame, yes, sir. Her heart is broken. It is your duty as Matt's best friend to make sure you and your family help her settle in. Such a lovely thing, too. To think she'll be living in that old, drafty house all by herself." The father shook his head.

Matt's house wasn't drafty. If anything, it was in better shape than his own. He could tell the good father was probably up to his old matchmaking schemes.

"And to think, the poor girl will be moving in all by herself, and in the state she's in, too. She could hardly shake my hand." Here it comes, he thought, as his gaze once again swept over to where the object of their conversation stood. She was now surrounded by half the town and looked very lost.

"You need to do the right thing by Matt and make sure his little sister gets settled in safely. God has some answers for her. She's come halfway across the world all alone to bury her poor brother." Father Michael shook his head. "I want you to promise me that you and your family will stop by the house often, you hear me?" he said with a sad look on his face.

Todd's gaze swept back to the priest. He knew that look. It was the same look he and a friend had gotten in high school after sneaking in to the cemetery with the Blake girls to try to scare them on Halloween night. The father had tried to scold them, but the entire time, he had been laughing at them, instead.

"Yes, Father," he murmured. Father Michael nodded his head and turned away to greet another group of people.

Todd looked back over at Megan and saw that she was even paler than before. He grabbed his sister's arm as she was walking past him and nodded in Megan's direction.

"Someone needs to go save her," he said under his breath.

"What do you suggest I do?" Lacey said with a stern look, placing both hands on her small hips.

"I don't know. You're the one who's good at breaking things…up," he added after his sister's eyes heated. Then he grabbed her shoulders and pointed her in Megan's direction.

He saw Lacey's shoulders slump a little after taking in the sight of Megan being swamped by the whole of Pride.

"Humph," Lacey grunted and started marching towards the growing crowd. His sister may be small, but she packed the biggest punch in town.

Megan stood there as an older gentleman talked to her. She hadn't caught his name when he'd barged to the front of the line and grabbed her hand.

"I didn't know Matt all that well, but he was a nice young man. He always had wonderful things to say about my bar, never once starting a brawl. Broke a couple up, though," the bar owner said with a crooked grin. "Always such a nice m-m-m," he started to stutter.

Concerned, she quickly looked up from the man's hand, which was tightly gripping her own. Standing beside the bar owner was a pixie. Megan didn't believe in fairy tales, but there was no other way to describe the woman. Megan had a strong urge to walk around the petite creature and see if wings were tucked under her dark purple raincoat. The woman was perfect, from the tip of her pixie-cut black hair to the toes of her green galoshes. Galoshes, Megan noted, that didn't have a speck of dirt on them. She was shorter than Megan and very petite with rounder curves. Her skin was fair and her eyes were a crystal gray blue. She had a cute nose that turned up slightly at the end and full lips that were a light shade of pink. She also had a commanding look on her face.

The bar owner literally backed away without even finishing his sentence, then he quickly walked away without so much as a glance back. Within seconds, everyone who'd gathered around her had wandered off, all without a single word from the pixie.

"How…?" Megan's voice squeaked, so she cleared her throat and started again, "How did you do that?"

"Well, it takes years of practice," the pixie said with a smile. "I'm Lacey Jordan." Her voice was smoky and laced with sexuality. "I was very good friends with your brother. I'm sorry he's gone."

The simple words touched something inside Megan. She could tell there was truth behind them. Lacey reached over and lightly grabbed Megan's good arm and then led her towards a row of parked cars.

"I'm also your neighbor. Shall we get you in out of the weather and home where you belong? We've made some meat pie for dinner, and I'm sure by the time we get there, the whole town will be right behind us. We'll go get my brothers and take you home."

"Oh, please, I don't want to be a bother. I'll be fine." Megan felt compelled to follow the small woman who still had a light hold on her arm and an air of command that surrounded her.

"Nonsense! It's no bother at all. Plus, if you turn down dinner," she said with a slight smile, "my brother Iian might get his feelings hurt. It's not every day he makes the family's famous dish." She continued walking towards the row of cars. "Come on then, let's get you out of this rain."

Megan looked up at the skies and at that exact moment, it started to lightly rain. Her mouth fell open in shock, but when a big fat drop landed on her bottom lip, she quickly closed it. Lacey was still lightly holding her arm and pulling her towards the parked cars near the side of the small white church.

Having not eaten before her flight to Portland, Megan felt her stomach growl. Exhaustion was settling in, and she felt a chill come over her bones. She wasn't sure what meat pie was, but if it had meat in it, she knew she could tolerate it.

"Oh! I'm sorry." She stopped walking, and Lacey turned and looked at her. "I forgot to mention that I have a rental car over there." She pointed slightly with her injured arm towards a small white sedan that she'd hastily rented at the airport four hours earlier.

"Give me the keys and my brothers can drive it over to the house for you," Lacey said, waving towards a man who had the same rich black hair. He'd been standing towards the back of the buildings in the shadows, so far back that Megan hadn't even noticed he was there.

As he stepped out, she saw that his hair was longer than his sister's. The man strolled over, appearing to be in no hurry, and he looked like he rather enjoyed the nasty weather and his surroundings. To say that he was tall would be an understatement; he must have been six and half feet and it only took him a couple of strides to reach where they stood.

Megan had to crane her neck to look up into his face, and she noticed that he had the same light eyes as his sister. His chin was strong with a tiny cleft, and his lips held a lazy smile that made him look rather harmless. Lacey handed him the keys to the rental car, then waved her hands in a sequence of patterns in front of her.

Lacey turned back to her. "Megan, this is my brother Iian. He's hearing impaired and uses sign language to communicate, but he can also read lips really well," she said while continuing to sign. Then turning her face away from his she said, "He likes to eavesdrop, so be careful what you say while facing him."

Smiling, Megan turned back to Iian in time to see the quick flash of humor in his eyes as he signed something to his sister. She gestured something back to him and hit him on the shoulder in a sisterly way.

"Come on, Megan. Iian will take care of your car." They began walking towards the cars as the rain came down harder. Groups of people without umbrellas were quickly sprinting to their vehicles. Others with umbrellas were making their way more slowly.

When Megan sank into the passenger seat of Lacey's sedan, chills ran up and down her spine. Lacey got in behind the wheel and started the engine. She turned the heater on full blast, and as it started to warm the inside of the car, Megan felt she could happily fall asleep right there.

They pulled away from the small church and the now-empty cemetery. The windshield wipers were clearing the rain from her view with a soft squeak, but Megan still felt like she wasn't able to see much beyond the path that the headlights were cutting through the fog. Then she sat up a little straighter and looked over at Lacey, who had her eyes on the road. Realizing she had just gotten into a stranger's car, she tensed. What did she really know about this small woman?

"You don't need to worry," Lacey said, not taking her eyes off the road. "I'm not going to kidnap you." She turned her head slightly and smiled. "We'll deliver you to your brother's house before everyone else gets there. I hope you don't mind, but we invited a few close friends over for potluck. It's what Matt would have wanted, something small. Your brother was very well liked around town, and people will want to bid him goodbye in this manner." She smiled sadly.

"Of course." She relaxed a little and rested her head against the window, enjoying the soft hum of the engine and the gentle beat of the wipers. By the time they pulled off the main road, the sky was dark; the sun hadn't come back out before setting for the night.

"Here we are now." Lacey parked the car so the headlights hit the house full force. "Matt spent most of the first year remodeling the place. I think you'll like what he's done with it." Lacey smiled at her.

Looking through the car window, Megan saw a large, white two-story house. Long green shutters sat on either side of picture windows that lined the whole front of the house. The front door was bright red with a brass knocker, and there were stained-glass windows on either side of the door. The windows seemed to glow brightly in the night.

Following Lacey's lead, she opened her door, and together they raced for the front porch through the light rain. Standing on the huge, brightly lit covered porch, she watched Lacey open the front door with a key from her own key chain. As they crossed the threshold, Megan's rental car pulled up in the driveway and parked next to Lacey's sedan.

Watching from the doorway, she saw Iian step out of the car along with the silver-blue-eyed man she had seen in the cemetery. Both men looked up to the front door and nodded to her and then stepped behind the rental car and started pulling her overnight bags from the trunk.

"They'll get those. Come on inside out of the cold," Lacey said. She walked towards the back of the house, leaving Megan standing alone in her brother's doorway.

Even though her brother had lived here for several years, she'd never visited Oregon before today. There had always been a reason not to visit him. Looking down at the cast on her arm, she realized that this was the reason she'd put off the last visit. The broken arm had been one more thing she had hidden from her brother, and she wished that she hadn't postponed that last trip.

Quickly turning into the house, she tried to avoid thinking about her brother and her regrets. Lacey was walking back towards her from the back of a long hallway, rubbing her hands together for warmth.

Just then, both men walked onto the front porch and shook their heads like dogs, shaking the rain from their hair. They wiped their feet on the wire mat before crossing into the entryway.

Megan noted that their faces were very similar, yet she could see subtle differences in the men. Their height and weight for one. Iian was slightly taller, with a broader build. And although the brothers shared the same gorgeous eyes, it was the depth of the one brother's that captured her attention again.

"Megan, this is my older brother, Todd," Lacey said from behind her.

Todd nodded his hello and looked at her, causing warmth to spread throughout her.

"It's chilly in here. Will you please start a fire in the living room before the guests arrive?" Lacey asked him.

Again, a nod was his only reply, and then he turned and went into the dark room to the right without saying a word.

"Iian," Lacey said and signed along, "please take those up to Matt's room and start a fire up there."

Lacey walked away, turning on lights as she went. Iian jogged up the curved staircase that sat to the left of the entryway. He had her suitcase in one arm like it weighed nothing and had thrown her overnight bag over his shoulder. It had taken all of her strength to drag those two bags through the airport that morning. His hair was still dripping wet and he was humming to himself. Humming? Megan thought.

As everyone bustled around, starting fires and turning on lights, Megan stood in the main entryway. She felt useless all over again. Here she was standing in her brother's home, letting strangers take care of her. Hadn't she promised herself that she would take care of herself from now on? But she was so tired. She didn't think that letting these people help her out for one night would hurt.

Lacey came back into the entryway. "Come on, let's get you out of that wet coat." Lacey reached for the rain jacket as Megan flinched away. Slowly Lacey's hands returned to her side.

"I'm sorry," Megan began, looking down at her hands, not wanting to look Lacey in the eyes. "I'm just a bit jumpy and tired I suppose." She tried to smile. How could she explain she didn't like to be touched?

"No need to apologize," Lacey said, warmly. "You must be overwhelmed. I'm sure a bit hungry by now, too. At any rate, people will start arriving any minute, and I'm sure there will be lots of food." As Lacey finished those words, the doorbell rang. "Go on in and have a seat by the fire. I'll take care of this."

Lacey pointed Megan in the direction of the two French doors that Todd had disappeared through earlier. Slowly walking towards them, Megan listened as Lacey greeted a group of people. Not really wanting to deal with anyone yet, she slipped inside the softly lit room and sighed as she rested against the wall.

Todd was across the room, bent over a pile of wood in the fireplace, blowing on flames that had started on some crumpled papers. He'd removed his leather jacket, and she noticed that he was wearing a white dress shirt that was stretched taut over his muscular arms. Powerful, was the word that came to her mind. She was nervous around powerful, so instead of walking over to the warmth of the fire, she turned back towards the doorway and watched Lacey greet everyone.

She was about to walk out to the hall and try to find the kitchen, when she felt hands lightly placed on her shoulders. Out of reflex, she jumped and spun around, her hand raised in defense.

"Easy," Todd murmured. "Let me take your coat; you're soaking wet." He held his hands out as one would to a wounded animal.

Blushing, she said, "I'm sorry. You startled me." She hung her head and turned around so that he wouldn't see her face turning red. Her heart was racing and her hands started shaking. It still affected her, being touched.

Gently, he helped her out of her jacket, being extra careful around her right arm. He hung it next to his coat on an oak rack by the door. When he noticed Lacey watching from the doorway, he said to her, "She can eat by the fire. She's frozen."

Lacey nodded in agreement. "There's a TV tray over in the corner. Go on, I'll bring a plate of food in once it's heated."

Father Michael had just walked into the house and was standing in the doorway with a few other people. Todd nodded to them then quickly walked her back into the living room under several watchful eyes. His hand gently cupped her good elbow.

Megan followed him back towards the fireplace where the room was warmer. She held her hand out towards the fire. She hadn't realized how freezing she was until the warmth hit her, causing her hand to tingle.

"I'm sorry. I didn't realize how cold I was until now," she said nervously to the room. She knew Todd was still behind her but didn't wanted to turn and look at him just yet. Closing her eyes, she let out the breath she'd been holding since he'd touched her. She was nervous around him, around men. When he touched her, however featherlight it was, it was like a power surge rushing through her body. She'd been avoiding getting close to anyone for so long that she knew she was out of practice. Taking a deep breath, she turned to the quiet room.

"You have his eyes." He interrupted her thoughts. He stood right inside the doors, his hands buried deep in his pockets as he watched her.

Megan was about to say something, anything, but just then Iian came into the room with a smile on his face. He stopped and took one look at his brother and then at her and signed something quickly to Todd. She wasn't sure what he said, but Todd gave his brother a frustrated look and then walked out of the room without saying a word to either of them.

Iian walked over to her and took her hand in his and said in a rich, warm voice, "Megan, I am very sorry about Matt."

Gasping, she realized she wasn't aware he could speak.

He smiled slightly. "I can speak. I lost my hearing in an accident when I was eighteen. I don't do it very often; my brother and sister say I have the most annoying voice."

She could hear the little blunders he made with his voice, as if he was out of practice. But he had such a rich, deep voice, so much like his brother's.

Speaking slowly and making sure to keep her face directed at his, she said, "You have a wonderful voice, rich and warm. Thank you for taking care of my luggage and starting a fire upstairs."

He smiled, while still holding her hand in his warm one. "You're chilled. Come over and sit down." He pulled her towards a dark-colored couch near the fireplace. "Lacey is still greeting people, but I'm sure you'll have a plate of food in front of you in no time. I'll sit with you and keep you company until then."

Back in the kitchen, Todd was helping his sister with the food, but his mind was back in the living room. He'd guessed by the look in Megan's eyes and the way she had jumped at his light touch that someone had hurt her, and recently too. The look on her face was heartbreaking, and he didn't care to see it on Matt's little sister. He was glad she'd turned away when she had, so she couldn't see the sadness and anger that had come into his eyes. Had Matt known this was going on? What she'd been going through? He didn't think so, but that didn't keep him from wanting to hunt someone down for the pain they had caused her.

His sister had seen the look on his face; she always saw everything. She had shaken her head at him and discreetly signed to him not to look so serious, that he might scare her. He'd quickly dropped his eyes and hidden it. He'd been so concerned about her, he hadn't even realized that his face had shown it.

Earlier, he'd watched Megan when she'd gone to the fire. She had started to relax and had rolled her shoulders, showing him a hint of her long white neck. He'd felt a flash of desire so strong that he had winced. That was when Iian had entered the room and signed for him not to look so serious. Was he that serious of a person that both his siblings had to warn him about it in one day? He didn't want to scare Megan, but he couldn't control the way his emotions played out on his face.

His brother and sister had a way of seeing things for what they were, which always annoyed him. At this point, he couldn't even muster up enough strength to go in there and talk with his brother about his feelings. He knew he wouldn't get anywhere talking about it with Lacey, but he could at least hold his own with Iian.

Hearing people roam about the house, he could just imagine Iian and Megan in the other room talking. His brother had a way of making women feel very comfortable and at ease. Thinking about them getting together, he realized that maybe he did have enough strength to go talk to his brother about his feelings.

As he walked towards the kitchen door to go and do just that, Lacey stopped him with one word. "Don't."

He turned to her ready to argue, but she only smiled at him.

Quickly, he let his breath out in a loud puff.

"How is it that you can defuse any situation with that smile?" he said, pulling her into a hug. "You drive me nuts."

She sighed and hugged him back, resting her head on his chest. "Give her time, Todd. Let Iian talk to her a while. She's going to need to trust us. She's had it hard." Taking a deep breath and a step back, she grabbed a plate of food and handed it to him. "Now, go take this to her and no more strange looks!" She smiled as she pushed him out the door.

Every bone in his body said that his sister was right, but his blood was boiling so hot he wanted answers. Matt had been like a brother to him, not just his best friend. What hurt Matt, hurt him. He missed his friend and felt sad, angry, and lost about his death. He knew Matt would've wanted them to take care of Megan and so he was going to make sure she was taken care of, period.

He knew that his brother and sister felt the same way about her as he did. Megan was family now. But he couldn't deny the quick pull he'd felt when he looked into those sea green eyes of hers.

Chapter Two

By the time Todd brought her a plate of food, the room was full of strangers. Everyone had quickly greeted her and moved on, and she was sure Lacey had told them to keep it short. The rooms in the house were warming up and with all the food being brought in, the place was starting to smell like heaven.

As she found out, meat pie was nothing more than a large beef potpie. After eating two helpings, a scoop of potatoes, and some potato salad, and washing it all down with some tea, she felt almost human again. She hadn't realized she could eat so much; it must have been the long flight and stress. Maybe it was the weather?

She returned her plate to the kitchen, which was full of older women, and began to wander around the rooms. She heard a baby crying and children playing loudly down the hall. Enjoying the warmth she felt from the people around her, she stopped occasionally and chatted with someone. Most were polite and had nothing but nice things to say about her brother. Matt really had embedded himself in the small town.

A group of older women approached her, and she smiled at them. "We wanted to welcome you to town and tell you how sorry we are for your loss," the smallest woman said. She was shorter than Megan and a good deal thinner. Her brown eyes showed sympathy. The other two women chimed in. They were slightly larger, but otherwise looked very similar to the other woman. "We're the Henderson sisters. We work down at the library. I'm Hanna and these are my sisters Hester and Henrietta." All three women were dressed similarly in long, flowered skirts, with long sweaters covering their thin frames. "If you need anything at all, please let us know."

She nodded but before she could say anything, another sister piped in. It took almost fifteen minutes for the trio to run through their speech, which seemed planned ahead of time. They had talked in detail about the town and most of the people in it, and she had enjoyed every word.

She must have met more than two dozen people before everything started blurring together. Too many faces and names she knew she wouldn't remember, so she found a soft chair somewhere and sat down as music started playing in the next room.

Someone was playing a violin, and the sad song drifted softly in from the TV room. Leaning her head back, she closed her eyes as images of her brother flashed in her mind.

She recalled all the years it had been just the two of them, all the birthday parties he'd thrown for the little girl she had been. She thought of all the Christmas presents he'd bought and wrapped, placing them under small trees they had picked out together. She remembered him hovering over her when she was sick with the flu after attending a friend's slumber party. It seemed like it had always been Matt. She could only vaguely remember her mother and had an even harder time conjuring up an image of her father.

"I could have the room cleared out in under a minute," a cheery whisper came from above, interrupting her thoughts. Megan opened her eyes without moving her head; Lacey was leaning over her and looking down at her.

"Oh, I'm sorry." She sat up a little straighter. "I was enjoying the music."

"Todd plays well," Lacey said, giving Megan a hand up from the chair.

“Todd?” she asked. “Todd is playing that?”

Lacey nodded. “He’s been playing since before I was born. Natural talent; all the Jordan’s have it,” she said, pulling her towards the back room.

When they reached the hallway, Megan could hear a low male voice singing along with the slow tune. Looking around the room, she noticed Todd was playing next to an old piano that sat in the corner. Iian was facing his brother, singing along with the music.

Their eyes were locked on each other for timing. Talent didn’t begin to describe a deaf man who could sing like that.

“He only sings on special occasions. Your brother was deserving of it,” Lacey said, smiling a little. She walked over and stood next to her brothers, singing with a rich smoky voice. The song was unfamiliar to Megan but spoke of lost love. It was soothing and sad. She leaned against the door frame and let the music fill her.

When the song ended, another one began, and the room and hallway filled up quickly as people made their way from other parts of the house. The chairs and coffee tables were quietly moved aside as they packed into the space.

One of the elderly women sat at the piano as another song began playing. There was more singing, dancing, and clapping than Megan had ever witnessed. People she didn't know had come to celebrate her brother's life. It brought a slight smile to her lips and tears to her eyes knowing that so many people cared. Before she knew it, she was being pulled into a dance with Father Michael.

What seemed like hours later, she walked back into the kitchen. The only remaining people in the house were a few churchwomen chatting as they cleaned the kitchen. Iian and Todd were still somewhere in the house as well, cleaning. Lacey had left a half hour earlier, heading off to work, she'd said. Before she left, Megan had overheard her scold her brothers into helping tidy the place up.

Looking to avoid more conversation, she headed back to the living room. Iian was there clearing off the coffee table. He looked up and gave her a smile.

"Come and sit down," he said, patting the couch. It looked so inviting that she was drawn to it. "I'll get the fire going again before I head off to work," he said, signing along. She liked to watch his hands move. She would have to pick up some basic words so she didn't feel left out.

After stoking the fire, he turned back to her. She signed to him, "Thank you." She'd seen Lacey using the motion earlier. His eyebrows shot up and he gave her an "I'm impressed" look.

He walked over and sat next to her. It was easy to talk to him. For some reason, he made her feel at ease. No other man had done that to her except for

Matt. Derek had, at first, but she had never truly trusted him. She was starting to relax into an easy conversation with Iian when the hair on the back of her neck stood up.

Todd had listened to their conversation from the hallway. As little brother's go, Iian was pretty cool. He remembered the day that his dad had brought him home. Todd had just turned ten and he remembered thinking that he had gotten a little brother for his birthday. But there had been a price; they had lost his stepmother in the process.

Lacey and Iian's mother had been like a mother to him. She'd been very young when she'd married his dad. His real mother had left shortly after his second birthday, and he had only seen her once since then, at his father's funeral. He knew she was only hanging around to see if she had been left anything.

But now as Iian and Megan's conversation continued, a knot formed in his stomach. It made him uneasy, and he stepped inside the doorway. Her hair clip had loosened over the hours, which gave him a view of her long, slender neck. And what a lovely neck it was.

Just then, however, her back straightened and her whole appearance changed. Only a minute ago she was on the verge of sliding down the couch. Now, her back was straight and her hands were gripped together in her lap. She looked ready to jump out of her skin. She turned her head slightly towards him, and his eyes went to his brother.

Iian signed to him, “You’re going to scare her.”

Again he thought, *What kind of an ogre am I if my family has to constantly warn me not to scare her?*

He signed back, not looking in her direction, “Don’t you have to be at work?” When Iian threw up his hands in frustration and quickly signed his favorite dirty phrase, Todd gave his brother a lopsided grin and chuckled.

Megan saw that grin, and her heart skipped a beat. Seeing his face transform, she quickly lost the uneasy feeling she’d had a minute ago. As she started to relax against the couch, she took a soothing breath and almost melted into the warmth and softness.

“You shouldn’t go barefoot in the house this time of year,” Todd said gently, walking to the fire and adding another log. Then he moved over and handed her the quilt off the back of a chair.

"I'm sorry." She looked down at her feet. She hadn't even realized that she'd taken off her black heels. It must have been a while ago, because her feet were freezing and they felt like they'd been that way for quite some time. Quickly tucking the quilt around her legs, she said, "Thanks," and tried to smile back at him.

Iian looked between the two of them and shook his head. "I have to leave now. Good night, Megan," he said and signed along. She signed the movements for "Good night" back to him.

He leaned down and gave her a small kiss on the cheek, and she jumped a little at the touch. Megan reminder herself that it was just like what Matt used to do, so she gave it no other thought. However, when she met Todd's eyes, she could see something else cross his face. When Todd followed his brother out the door without saying a word, she settled back down to watch the flames.

"Good night, dear," she heard from behind her, causing her to jump. She had forgotten about the ladies from the kitchen. They shuffled into the room and quickly headed towards the front door. Megan moved to get to her feet.

"No, don't get up, we can see ourselves out. You've had a tiring day. After you get yourself settled in, we'll come for a nice long visit," a younger woman about Megan's age said.

Megan thought her name was Laura. She knew the woman was married with several kids who had all been taken home earlier by the woman's husband. Then there was Sue and Diana. They each had two children and seemed very nice. Megan had enjoyed seeing all the kids earlier. They had brightened her dark mood.

"You are well stocked with leftovers in the fridge, and we've cleaned and cleared everything. Have a restful evening. We do hope you'll be staying in Pride for good." Then the trio disappeared down the hallway, heading out the front door.

After she heard the door click shut, the same questions kept playing over and over in her head. She'd been asked numerous times that evening if she would be living in Pride now. Was she staying in town? Did she know that answer herself? She'd just settled back down and was enjoying the warmth as it spread throughout her body when she heard the floorboard creek behind her.

She was up in a flash, her body tensed, and all her sore muscles screaming. Todd stood right inside the doorway.

"I'm sorry," he said, holding up his hands. "I left my keys, there." He pointed to them. "On the table."

She blushed and, feeling like a fool, let her shoulders relax little by little. She could feel the tension leave her body, leaving behind a tingling trail. Her breath was coming faster than she wanted, so she deliberately took a deep breath and released it slowly through her nose. She found it hard to look at his eyes and chose instead to look at his hands, which were raised, palms up.

"I'm sorry, I'm a little tired," she said, never once taking her eyes from his hands. "New place, you know, new house and all."

He walked slowly towards her. "Megan, you don't have to explain anything to me. No one will harm you here," he said softly. "I'll lock the door behind me." He grabbed his keys, turned, and was gone.

She stood there looking at the empty doorway for a few minutes. Finally, she turned and shut the glass fireplace doors on the now dying fire. Taking the quilt with her, she began the climb to the second floor.

At the top of the stairs, she noticed there were two smaller bedrooms with a bath in between them. They each had queen beds, dressers, and small night tables. At the end of the hall was the master bedroom, which was as big as the other two rooms put together. It faced the back of the house and had lovely French doors that led to a deck. It was too dark outside to see how big the deck was, but she thought it was fairly large. Leaning her head against the glass doors, she could hear the rain.

The room itself was very comfortable and had a four-poster, king-size bed in the middle. There was a small writing desk off to one corner and two small night tables. One had a brightly lit alarm clock on it and the other held a plain white lamp. A picture of Megan and Matt sat next to the lamp. She walked over and picked it up.

She remembered the picture well; it had been taken on her wedding day. Matt had his arm around her waist, and they were both smiling. She remembered feeling on top of the world that day. She could see in his eyes that he'd been proud of her. Matt hadn't really had a chance to get to know Derek very well. She realized now that Derek had probably kept his distance on purpose.

She set the picture down and walked over to the door that was next to the fireplace. There was a bathroom with an oversized garden tub and a stand-alone shower. She wouldn't be able to use the shower for another few weeks due to her cast, so she leaned over the tub and started to fill it with warm water.

The fireplace was set into the wall opposite the tub, warming both rooms at once. She found some bubble soap in the cupboard by the mirror and poured a little into the tub.

Leaving the tub to fill, she headed back into the bedroom. She went into the walk-in closet and walked through, touching her brother's shirts.

Seeing one she remembered him wearing all the time, she took it off the hanger, pulled it up to her face, and breathed in her brother's smell. Her knees went weak, and she sank down to the floor of the closet and cried.

Chapter Three

The next day, Megan woke to birds singing. She hadn't slept straight through a night without fear in years. She felt like jumping out of bed until the memories came flooding back. There was a dull ache where her brother used to be, and a shooting pain running up her back and down her arm. But the sun was coming in through the curtains that covered the windows, and she could hear the birds singing outside.

Stretching her good arm above her head, she sat up and rolled her shoulders, trying to relax her bruised muscles. She tried to pull her tangled hair into a simple ponytail. She'd been tempted to chop it all off until she could use both arms again, but she supposed she was vain and wanted to keep it long. Walking over to the French doors, she moved the drapes aside and gasped at the view. She fumbled with the door locks then threw open the doors. She took in a deep breath of fresh air; she could smell a hint of lingering rain and grassy meadows.

"Oh, Matthew, it's beautiful," she whispered.

It was February in Oregon, so the air held a chill, but she could see the sun behind a thin layer of fog, which was quickly disappearing. The fields behind the house were so green it almost hurt her eyes. Stepping out on the deck, she saw that it covered the entire side of the house. There were stairs leading down to the backyard, and she could see birds perched on the huge old tree that shaded the back of the house.

She loved the sound of them and smiled as they flew from tree branch to tree branch. She thought about getting some birdseed when she went into town for supplies. She could just make out the ocean, which peeked through the thick trees at the edge of the field next to the barn. A brown garage and an even bigger red and white barn stood off to the side of the house. The garage looked like it was in need of a fresh coat of paint. Through the open doors, she could see a black Jeep. The barn looked like it could use some repair as well, but for the most part, both were in fairly good shape.

Turning back into the room, she glanced at the clock on the nightstand. It couldn't be eleven o'clock! She was sure it had been around midnight when she'd finally crawled into bed and gone to sleep. She hadn't slept this much in a long time.

Walking over to her suitcase, she pulled out an old pair of jeans and put them on. She started to pull out one of her shirts, but changed her mind and instead walked over to the closet and pulled out one of Matt's favorite shirts. She put it on over her tank top. It was soft and smelled of her brother. She pulled on a pair of her brother's thick, wool socks, quickly made the bed, and went downstairs.

When she reached the bottom step, she stopped and listened. The place felt cold and empty, and she realized that she hadn't lived in a house since her parents' death. They had always rented apartments, never houses. Then when she had moved out on her own, she'd lived in the college dorms until she'd purchased a small townhouse with Derek.

This was a house. A very large house. There was even a chandelier in the main entryway, hanging from the top floor over the twisted staircase. The windows on either side of the door let in plenty of sunlight, which made the entryway bright and cheerful.

Turning to the left, she looked into what she thought was her brother's study. The blinds were closed in the room, so she reached for a light switch. There was an oak desk that sat in the middle of the room and she noticed that it was clean, with not a piece of paper out of place.

The floors throughout the entry and office were a light oak. They shined and she could tell that they were well maintained. An ornamental rug covered most of the office floor, making it feel warm and cozy. A dark leather couch sat next to a small fireplace with bookcases on either side of it. All of the shelves were neatly stacked with books. There was a bay window in the opposite wall with a cushioned window seat covered by small pillows. There wasn't a thing out of place in the room and it reminded her so little of Matt.

She'd really been in too much of a daze yesterday to have given the house and rooms any thought. Would she stay here? Would she sell the place? At this point, she didn't even want to think about it.

Heading back down the hall, she passed a formal dining room with a maple table and twelve chairs; they had been filled with people she hardly knew only last night.

At the end of the hallway was a wide door. She pushed it open and stepped into the kitchen. It was as tidy as the rest of the house. It looked bright and cheery today with white curtains hanging over the windows that overlooked the backyard. The room was beautiful. There was an oversized white oven that filled one wall, and brass pots hung from hooks over a marble island. Fresh flowers had been placed on the table. Again, the place looked cleaner than she knew Matt had probably ever kept it thanks to the churchwomen who had worked hard last night.

Back down the hallway was a large sitting room with a couple of comfortable looking chairs and a cozy couch. The back wall was covered with more bookcases and a stone fireplace. Books covered the shelves from ceiling to floor, some sitting in front of others, stacked in disarray. The small standing piano stood against the wall. Her brother had learned to play at a young age and had always tried to teach her. Tried, but never really succeeded.

Her brother had always loved books, sometimes reading for hours with no breaks. This was the room her brother had spent most of his time in, and she could imagine him sitting in front of the fire with a book. Walking over to the shelves, she picked a book at random and sat down to a quiet house.

It wasn't long before she heard a knock at the door, which almost caused her to drop her book. Shaking a little, she started to get up from her comfortable spot when she heard keys rattling and the front door opening.

"Megan, it's Lacey," she heard through the haze of her mind. Still shaking, she quickly took deep calming breaths and called out, "I'm back here."

Sitting again, she continued to slow her breathing so that when Lacey appeared in the doorway, the shaking had gone and her breath was under control.

Lacey was dressed in what Megan assumed was her uniform for work. The fitted black pants were pressed, and she wore a red and white striped shirt that had a nametag on her lapel. She carried a pan covered with tinfoil. Megan's mouth started to water when the smells reached her. She realized that she was starving.

"I hope you don't mind; Matt gave us all keys. I stopped by earlier but didn't think you were awake yet. I hope you slept well. I wanted to bring over some hot cinnamon rolls, one of my specialties, before I headed out to work. I brought over all the rolls I could sneak away from my brothers." Lacey smiled as she nodded for Megan to follow her back to the kitchen. "Do you know that Iian can eat a dozen of these in one sitting?" She laughed. "How he can do that and look like he does is a mystery to me."

Megan chuckled and followed her into the kitchen. Noticing the book that Megan was carrying, Lacey chimed in, "I know your brother has a vast collection of books, but if you get bored and want to get outside, you might want to take a look at the cabins."

"Cabins?" Megan sat down, placing the book on the table.

Lacey nodded her head. "There are five of them. Your brother wanted to start renting them out, like a bed-and-breakfast. They sit on the same path that takes you down to the beach." As Lacey pulled out a plate, she pointed out the kitchen window. "That path there. I know Matt, Iian, and Todd did a lot of work on the cabins, but I don't think they finished everything. The keys are on the hook right inside that cupboard." She pointed and then started scooping a very large cinnamon roll onto a plate. "I know you're still unsure whether you want to stay here, but take a look, take a walk, and maybe it will help you make the decision."

Handing Megan the plate, Lacey took a plate for herself and sat down next to her at the table. Lacey had an uncanny way of saying what Megan was feeling. She'd been staying inside, avoiding decisions. Maybe a walk is what she needed. Megan took a bit of the sweet, warm rolls.

"There should be a law against these." Megan smiled over at Lacey. "I think I could eat a dozen of them myself. But don't expect me to stay thin."

Lacey smiled. "Why do you think I brought them over here? So I wouldn't be tempted to eat them all myself." They both laughed.

After Lacey left, Megan dug some walking shoes out of her suitcase and grabbed a heavy coat from her brother's closet. Setting out with the keys in her pocket, she walked down the winding path that Lacey had pointed out.

Wildflowers and tall grass grew along the path, which was covered with small round pebbles. Even in the cold, the flowers were flourishing. It took her less than five minutes to wind around the trail and come to the clearing that housed the first cabin.

It was small and had a wooden porch and a bright blue door with the number one on it. Taking her keys out, she used the blue key with that number on it. Matt had always liked bright colors.

The place smelled of fresh paint and varnish. The empty rooms echoed with each footstep she took. It was very clean and fresh looking, and she could see the potential that it held. The walls were painted a warm honey color that accentuated the oak of the floors and the trim. The windows were huge and gleamed in the sunlight.

She walked towards the back and opened a heavy wood door into a small room that she imagined would easily fit a double bed and two nightstands. Turning to the left, she walked into a small bathroom with no toilet or tub. There were places for them, but they hadn't been installed yet.

Yes, there was a lot of potential here. It took her almost an hour to go through all five cabins, each one larger than the one before, until finally she reached the fifth and final cabin. It was not only the largest, but the least completed. Its windows and porch overlooked the beach. A short walk down a hill and across a small field of sand covered in tall green grass and you would be down at the water's edge.

The last two cabins were unpainted, and the floors, trim, and doors still needed to be sanded and stained. None of the cabins had appliances. Where the first three cabins were small with only a front room, a small bedroom, and a bath, the last two had two bedrooms, good-sized bathrooms, and small kitchenette areas. The countertops and cabinets needed replacing or sanding.

Yes, she could definitely see why her brother wanted to start a business renting these out. The buildings were made to have families, friends, and lovers enjoy them. Standing on the front porch of the last cabin, she imagined honeymooners having a romantic dinner out here, or a family eating a picnic after a day at the beach. She imagined them playing volleyball in the field on the way to the beach. She could envision a few picnic tables along the path, all painted to match the brightly colored doors her brother had taken the time to paint.

Her brother's dream was slowly becoming her own.

A few days later, for the first time since arriving, she stood in the kitchen making her own dinner. Thank goodness there had been several cans of tomato soup in the pantry and a bag of frozen vegetables in the freezer. She even found an unopened box of Wheat Thins. Not only was this one of the more elaborate meals she knew how to make, but one of her favorites. She had enjoyed having people stop by and visit the last few days, and she knew they meant well, but she had missed the quiet of being alone.

After setting a bowl and a plate of crackers down on the white tablecloth, she enjoyed her quick meal, thinking how peaceful it was. Could she really get used to strangers coming and going around here? She had a skittish personality, but she hadn't always been like this. For most of her life with Matt, she hadn't been scared. She knew people were generally good and it appeared that the people of Pride took care of each other.

As she finished rinsing her dishes, she saw Lacey's sedan drive up and park in front of the garage. Going to the back door and opening it, she waited for her friend. When Todd stepped out of the car instead, she tensed slightly. Forcing herself to put a smile on her face and relax, she welcomed him.

"Hi, Megan. I hope you don't mind, but I needed to pick up some paperwork from your brother's office. While I was here, I figured I would take a look at the downstairs bathroom sink. Lacey said she noticed that the handle was loose the last time she was here." He grabbed a toolbox from the back of the car.

"Oh, I don't want to bother you. I'm sure I can figure it out myself."

"It's no trouble. I helped Matt install that sink less than a year ago. If you're busy, I can come back later," he said, looking up the three stairs at her.

She realized she was blocking the back door and quickly moved aside. "No, I'm sorry, please." She motioned him in.

"It will only take me a few minutes and then I'll be out of your way." He headed down the hall towards the bathroom.

She walked into the living room and placed another log on the fire. She paced in front of the fireplace, feeling tense and uneasy as she waited for him to finish up.

After about ten minutes, she sat down and picked up the book she had started earlier that day. She knew she shouldn't be reading a Stephen King book, especially with her nerves, but she just couldn't put it down. She'd always loved a good scary story. Probably her brother's doing.

Just then the floor board behind her creaked and she jumped once again.

"I'm sorry," Todd said with a reassuring smile. "I was going to tell you that I was done. I'll be heading out now."

She couldn't, just couldn't, look him in the eyes again, so she bent over to pick up the book that she'd dropped. Instantly, she winced from the pain. The bruised muscles that ran from her shoulders to her lower back were flaring up again. Gasping, she reached out for something, anything, for support.

Todd was next to her in a second. "Easy," he murmured. "Did you hurt your neck? Here now, let me see," he said, walking her backwards towards the couch. At the same time, he took a light hold on the neckline of her baggy shirt to reveal her slender neck.

"It's nothing, just..." Megan tensed again and started to pull away, but his hands remained lightly on her shoulders.

"I'm not going to hurt you. Let me help you. Your shoulders must be sore, carrying the weight of that cast around all day," he said in a soft voice, holding her steady. "I want to help you. Trust me." She turned slightly and looked up into his eyes. Seeing his concern, all she could do was nod in reply.

He lightly tugged her shirt to the side, exposing her neck and half of her right shoulder. She heard his gasp, and looked back over her shoulder at him. When she saw the raw emotions flash across his face, she tensed.

Pulling away, she backed up until the backs of her legs hit the couch. "I...I'm sorry." She moved farther away. He walked over to her, and she became trapped in his eyes. She felt like her feet were glued to the floor. She could no longer see hurt and anger in his eyes, only concern.

Todd closed his eyes, taking several deep breaths to calm himself. When he had looked down at Megan's skin, he'd been shocked. He had expected her skin to be a soft creamy color just like her lovely neck, but it was covered in deep purple and green bruises that crossed her shoulders. Reaching out with just his fingers, he gently played them over her neck and shoulder, like whispers on her skin.

Getting in control again, he masked the emotions that had played across his face. He wanted to rip apart the person who had hurt her. Knowing he had to keep his emotions under control for her sake, he kept them tightly tucked inside. She'd turned around and not taken her eyes from his face. He could tell she was waiting for his next move.

He slowly pulled the large shirt from her shoulders. Pulling it over the cast gently, he bunched it up and tossed it on the couch. When she started to object, he cooed to her, "Let me look. I won't hurt you, just let me see."

Pushing the light strands of her white tank top aside, he exposed more bruised skin. He lightly took her shoulders in his hands and turned her around so he could view her back.

She leaned her head farther down, exposing all of her neck to him. The bruises started at each shoulder and went below her shirt. He could see deep purple and blackish-green skin through the light material. Large, ugly, bruises ran down the back of both of her arms.

After about a minute of silence, he stalked from the room, leaving her alone facing the fire.

When he came back in, her eyes were fixed on the floor and he could see tears streaming down her soft cheeks. Then he looked down at what her eyes were fixed on.

"No wonder you're on edge, reading this," he said, picking up the discarded book.

He stood in front of her with a book in one hand and bottle of dark liquid in the other. She kept her head down, looking at his hands.

Dropping the book on the couch, he put his fingers under her chin and pulled her face slowly up until their eyes met. "Here now, don't," he said wiping her tears away gently.

"I'm sorry…" she started to apologize.

"Don't, please. Will you let me help you? This will help with the sore muscles and bruises." He held out the bottle, letting her see the label. "Trust me, I've had plenty of both." He smiled a little.

Megan nodded.

"Come on then, sit down here." He pointed to the couch.

She followed him and sat at the edge of the couch with her back to him.

"Lay down, Megan," he said softly.

He lifted her shirt to the point that half of her back was exposed. She heard him take a deep breath and she tensed again.

"No, don't. It's alright," he said.

She could smell the ointment as he warmed it in his hands. He started working on her shoulders first, the muscles screaming from the contact.

"Take deep breaths," he said in a soothing voice, relaxing her tension. "When I was about thirteen, I decided I was man enough to help break one of my dad's horses, Thunder, an Appalachian. It had been terribly mistreated before we got ahold of him. I snuck into his pen one day, thinking I would just jump right up there, and we would be best of friends." He chuckled. "Well, everything was going fine until my dad came running out of the house screaming. The horse took one look at him and bucked me right off. I flew over the fence and landed backside down in the blackberry bushes. I can still remember my dad's face as I went flying." He chuckled a little, but continued to rub slowly. "He tore those bushes out the next day and sold the horse to a farmer." He laughed to himself again.

Even after all that, his back hadn't looked as bad as hers did now. His smile faded.

Working his way up and down her battered back, he wondered what had happened to her. Had Matt know anything about this? No! He was sure his friend hadn't known what his sister was going through. Matt was a lot like him; he would have wanted blood it he had known this was happening to someone he cared about—or, for that matter, someone he hardly knew.

Todd felt some responsibility where Megan was concerned because Matt wasn't here to do it. After all, Matt had been his best friend for the last four years. Matt had helped him deal with the loss after his father's death and the responsibilities that came along with having a younger brother and sister who relied on him. Iian had just turned eighteen and Lacey had been twenty, but there had been plenty of responsibilities he'd had to deal with when he'd taken over the family's businesses.

"Tell me about Boston," he said, trying to get her to relax under his hands. She was small, and the muscles in her back were knotted and twisted. The bruises ran further down her back to below her pants, but he stayed well above that line.

He could tell that she was starting to feel more comfortable; the ointment was warm, and his hands were warmer. He could feel her muscles relaxing one at a time. She started telling him about Boston, where she and Matt had grown up.

Matt had been born here in Oregon, but she'd been born in Maine almost fifteen years later. When she was two, their parents had moved to Boston so their dad could start his own law firm there. He'd always been very strict with his children.

His hands were slowly soothing away all the aches, and he could feel her relaxing into them. Electrified was the best word to describe how he felt around her. He had felt connected to her from the first glance and had chalked it up as a good, wholesome dose of lust. Nothing wrong with that, right?

She was beginning to mumble as she told him about her old job in Boston. Her words were starting to slur together, then she said, "Tell me about yourself, your family. Lacey said you own a restaurant."

"Yes. The Golden Oar has been in our family for several generations. Lacey and Iian really run the place now. I run our other business, which my dad started, Jordan Shipping. Actually, your brother was my business partner," he said, stroking her neck. "We have a small fleet of ships that go to every continent." As he continued to tell her the details of his company, he heard her breathing slowing down and becoming shallow. Then, she was asleep.

Shifting lightly, he grabbed the quilt off the back of the couch and covered her from neck to toe. He banked the fire, made sure the front door was locked, and walked out the back one, locking the dead bolt with the set of keys Matt had given him.

On his drive home, he couldn't get the bruises and marks on her back out of his mind.

"What am I supposed to do with your sister?" he asked as he drove home. He didn't expect Matt to answer, but he felt better for trying.

Tomorrow he would have to call an old buddy, a private investigator who lived in New York. Todd needed some answers and he knew Mark was the one who could get them for him.

Chapter Four

Megan settled into a schedule over the next few days, usually waking up early to work around the house or out in the yard whenever the weather permitted. She was trying to clear a patch of yard so she could plant a small garden. At least once a day, there was a Jordan over at the house. Yesterday, Lacey had brought another batch of her cinnamon rolls. She had stayed around to chat for over an hour. Megan was becoming accustomed to the company dropping by and felt, really felt, like part of something bigger.

She found the little grocery store in town quite enchanting. The plump owner, Patty O'Neil, whom she'd met at Matt's funeral, always talked her ear off about the town and everyone in it.

Usually she didn't mind, but today she felt trapped there, listening to the woman as she stood at the register. All of her items were bagged and paid for, but she could think of no polite way to get away trapped there listening to the woman with no real polite way out. She could imagine her double chocolate macadamia nut ice cream melting by the second. She even thought about dropping the groceries and running. There really wasn't a lot of food in the two small bags, since she and cooking didn't really mix.

But she really did want some of that ice cream. The way it was going, she was going to have to drink it instead of savoring it slowly like she'd dreamed.

"So that's how Robert became sheriff. Quite the young gun he was back then until he settled down and married Amelia…" Megan had zoned out during most of the conversation. "That's Betty, poor dear. Lost her Henry last year," she said, nodding out the window to a small older woman walking towards the store. Megan recognized her as one of the ladies who'd stopped by the day after her brother's funeral.

"Hi, Betty," Patty said as the woman walked in the double doors. "How are you feeling today?"

"Oh, my arthritis is acting up again, but I'm doing fine. Hello, Megan. We really weren't introduced the other day. I'm Betty Thomas. I help out at all the church events. Kind of the coordinator, if you will."

"Betty bakes some of the finest cakes in all of Oregon," Patty said. "She brought her angel food cake with the chocolate frosting to your place last week."

"Yes, it was very good. I think I had two pieces," Megan said.

"We're so glad you'll be staying on. You know, we have weekly prayer meetings at my house. I do hope to see you there," Betty said.

"Well, the thing is, I'm not Catholic," Megan said with a weak smile. She didn't want to get into the fact that she hadn't completely made up her mind to stay, yet.

"Oh," they both said in unison, sounding rather put out. "Well," Betty said recovering, "that's alright. You could come anyway. It must be hard moving in with that hurt arm. How did you say you broke it?" There was an awkward silence that filled the room, and both women leaned ever so slightly forward.

Megan looked around the store and saw four other women standing behind her in line, their buggies stacked with forgotten melting items, and no one seemed to mind. They were all ears; she could imagine them holding their breath, waiting for the scoop.

"We had a bad ice storm in Boston a few weeks back, and I fell outside my apartment. The Jordan's helped me move in. They've been very helpful the last few days." The statement flew from her lips faster than she had wanted. She was sure that the false news of how she broke her arm would spread around town before nightfall.

"Well, now, I remember Matt saying that you were married. Is your husband still in Boston?" She was getting the feeling that Betty was not only the best baker in town, but the best gossip as well.

She looked from woman to woman, not wanting to take this conversation any further, feeling trapped and starting to feel light-headed from hunger. She'd gone to the store in the first place because her house was empty of food.

When she felt like she would pass out from hunger, she looked outside the windows and saw Lacey walking towards the building, her small form traveling remarkably fast.

"There you are!" Lacey said after swinging the door wide. "I've been looking all over for you." She looked at Megan and Patty and the other women in line, all of whom quickly looked away and went about their business. "We better get going or you're going to be late."

She was saved! She could have kissed Lacey for rescuing her. Lacey grabbed one of her bags and walked out the door without even so much as a "Hello" to the other women.

"I really need to learn how to do that," she said, walking behind her and trying to catch up.

Lacey chuckled and put the bag into Megan's trunk. Then she reached over and took the other bag and set it down. "It's easy. You'll get used to everyone around here. You should just ignore the gossiping bunch. If you don't know by now, Betty Thomas is one of the biggest in town."

"After what just happened in there, I can believe it." They were both laughing as they turned and saw the women looking back at them through the glass.

"You know, maybe you can clear something up for me?" Megan asked.

"Shoot," Lacey said.

"Miss Gossip in there mentioned the bed-and-breakfast, and it got me thinking about Matt. I know my brother, and I just can't see it. Do you know why he wanted to do something like that?"

Lacey had a questioning look on her face.

"Megan, your brother was not only really excited about opening the bed-and-breakfast, he had serious plans to convince you to move out here and help him. Maybe this is something we can talk about when your ice cream isn't running out of your bag," she said, holding up a small paper bag with chocolate running out the sides. "How about I swing by after my dinner shift. I'll bring dessert, since it appears your ice cream is now soup."

Lacey arrived right before dark. True to her word, she carried a plate of desserts they served at the restaurant. The triple chocolate cheesecake was Megan's favorite. She felt guilty for eating both pieces that Lacey had brought.

"Maybe you can clear something else up for me," she said, chewing her lip with worry. "Betty also mentioned something that I didn't quite understand about Todd's first wife." Megan left the question open, waiting.

Lacey looked up from her cake. "Sara." She set down her fork. "They were married for almost two years when she became pregnant. Almost a month into the pregnancy, the doctor noticed something wrong with her blood test. They had a choice: treat the cancer and lose the baby, or try to go full term and treat the cancer after. In the beginning of her third trimester, she went in for a checkup, and they put her in the hospital, where she stayed for almost two weeks before we lost them both." Lacey looked up into Megan's eyes.

"Losing someone like that, it does something to you. If it hadn't been for your brother, Todd wouldn't be the man you see today. Matt saved my brother. No, Matt saved my whole family. Less than a year later, we lost our dad and Iian lost his hearing. It was Matt that helped us get back in the swing of life. It was your brother who helped us see that we could go on. I know that if he was here, he would say the same to you."

Megan stiffened. Lacey reached over and took her hand. "Please don't pull away. I won't pry. But your brother saved us, and all three of us feel the same way about you that we did about him. You're our family now, part of us."

Wiping a tear from her cheek, Megan took a deep breath. "Tell me your thoughts about Matt's bed-and-breakfast idea." She'd been going over it in her head all day. The business plan sounded solid, but she had never run her own business before, just marketed others.

Lacey smiled. "I know that Iian was more a part of it than anyone. I think they had come up with a business plan. I'm sure there are printouts and spreadsheets somewhere in the office." Lacey scooped up the last bit of a yellow cake.

"I always liked the idea; the cabins are a perfect setting for a romantic getaway or a family fun weekend. They're very close to the beach, which is a great bonus for bringing people in. Pride is the kind of place people love to visit and currently the only place to stay is the Motel 8, which is seven miles out of town and always full of truckers. Not a very nice place for vacationers." Setting the plate aside, she scooted closer. "What are your plans, Megan?"

"I, well, I really hadn't given it much thought. I had planned on coming out here to stay with Matt until I was back on my feet. Maybe find a job in Portland. That was before this." She lifted her arm. "But I didn't want to burden Matt. I didn't want to upset him. He had always done so much for me; I couldn't let him down like that. But before I could heal and get here..."

"Megan," Lacey said, waiting until her friend looked her in the eyes. "Nothing you could have ever done would have made your brother think less of you. He was always so proud of you, and I believe even now he would be proud of you." Tears formed in Megan's eyes again, and Lacey bent over and gave her a hug. "I think we need some of my melted ice cream to wash this cake down," Megan said. And even though she didn't say it, at that moment they both knew that she was going to stay in Pride.

When the sun finally made an appearance a few days later, Megan decided to take another look at the cabins. She took a pad of paper and a pencil with her this time and wrote down everything that needed to be done. There were really only two cabins that still needed a bit of work. . She had painted rooms before and always found it relaxing.

She knew nothing about the electrical and plumbing and would need to hire a contractor to make sure everything was up to date. She would need someone to help paint and do the floors. She had painted rooms before and always found it relaxing, but the cast on her arm would make it difficult. Megan took notes for each cabin, scribbling as best she could with her left hand.

When she was done, she stood on the porch of the largest of the cabins, enjoying the wonderful view of the beach. She decided to head down to the surf and took the path that had been cut out of the tall grass. The beach itself was beautiful and private, and would make a perfect place for visitors to enjoy. Even on cold days, its charm outweighed the chill. She walked up and down the beach, enjoying the quiet and the fresh air.

She was humming a happy tune several hours later when she walked back to her front porch and saw Iian sitting in one of the wicker chairs, smiling back at her.

"Hi," she said and sat down next to him, turning her body so that he could easily read her lips.

"Visiting the cabins?" he asked. When she nodded, he continued. "What did you think?"

"Oh, they are quite lovely. I think you and Matt were right. They would be perfect to rent out. They only need a little work." She handed him her list. He chuckled at her writing, but read over it. As he looked down at the paper, she noticed how strong his profile was. He was quite different from his brother, not only in looks, but in the fact that she felt very comfortable around him. When Todd was around her, she was full of butterflies.

When he was done reading the list, he looked up at her. "I'm very impressed. Matt and I had come up with almost the same list. Come, I'll show you." He stood and held out his hand to help her up from the chair. She hesitated for a second, then put her hand in his larger one and walked into the house. Iian went into the office and pulled out a file from the cabinet that sat on the left side of the desk.

He set the file on the desk and motioned for her to sit. She sat in the soft leather chair and pulled open the file. Matt had done his homework alright, down to the contractor's bids for the work and the color of the walls. He had even ordered furniture for each cabin. There were receipts in the file for the work done on the smaller three cabins that were almost completed. Holding the receipts, she looked up at Iian.

He smiled and said, "The furnishings are already at the warehouse, ready to be delivered when the work is done. Matt, Todd, and I had been doing a lot of the work ourselves, but here is the list of contractors we used for the rest." He pointed to a bid and said, "I'm sure he would be happy to add more work to this. As for the landscaping, well, there's a place outside of town…" He trailed off.

"Oh, I could do that easily. I love working with…" Megan trailed off. She realized she wasn't facing him and there was no way Iian would be able to read her lips. She blushed and turned back to him and repeated her statement. "I have quite the green thumb. I have some really good ideas, too. Of course, I would have to get familiar with what kinds of plants are best for around here."

He smiled one of those quick, heart-stopping smiles. "Pretty much anything grows that you put in the ground. Matt said you were good with making things grow, and I kind of figured you would want to take care of that part. You know," he said, walking over and sitting on the couch, "since the cabins aren't equipped with full kitchens, you could provide meals here in the main house. How are you with cooking?" he asked.

"Hmm," Megan said, frowning down at the paper. How could she tell him that she couldn't even fry an egg without fire departments in two counties standing by? "Well," she said, looking back at him, "not so good."

"That's okay," he jumped in. "Lacey and I can help in that department. We'd talked about making it a joint venture as far as the meals go."

"How so?" she asked leaning forward.

"Well, The Golden Oar would provide the breakfast and lunch—sandwiches and soups." He waved his hands about.

"We could provide special discount rates to your customers for dinners. Of course, this could all be worked out later, but Matt had come up with the idea about helping each other out. We would have advertisements on the back of our menus for your cabins, and the extra customers coming in for the discounts would help the restaurant out."

"That sounds like a great plan," she said, beginning to see the smart business plan her brother had put into motion.

"Have you given any thought to what you might want to call it?" he asked.

"Had Matt?" she asked with a smile.

He smiled back. Standing up, he walked back to the file cabinet. Pulling out a folder, he set in on the desk in front of her.

Megan slowly opened it and blinked in surprise. There in front of her was an artist's rendering of her and Matt smiling in front of one of the cabins with the ocean behind them. "Pride Bed-and-breakfast" was printed across the top. It was an impressive sketch of the two of them taken from a picture before Megan had married. It brought tears to her eyes seeing that Matt had thought of her and made her a part of this.

Megan remembered one of the last conversations she'd had with her brother. No wonder he'd been so insistent on her coming out here to visit him. He had planned all along on her being his partner.

She, however, had been going through her own private hell and had kept putting off the visit. Guilt sank in and she kept her eyes focused on the paper.

"He had hoped that you would move out here to be closer to him," Iian said, leaning over her shoulder and looking down at the picture of his friend. "He loved you very much. He would have done anything for you. You know, we viewed your brother as part of our family. Since he never stopped talking about you, we view you as part of the family as well."

"Thank you," Megan said, shaking her head and wiping her tears. She smiled back up at him. "I think I would rather enjoy having you as a…" She didn't get any further. Iian had stopped looking at her and had glanced up towards the door. Megan turned her head to see what had taken his attention away.

Todd stood right inside the doorway, his fists balled by his sides. He had a fierce look on his face and was staring at his brother like he wanted to tear him apart. Todd quickly signed in jerked motions to his brother. Megan was starting to shake and feel uncomfortable around the display of anger. Iian signed something back to Todd, and his whole attitude changed and he became very relaxed. Todd shoved his hands in his jeans pocket and walked back out the door without another word. Megan could hear him pacing on the front porch.

"I'm sorry, what was that all about?" Megan asked, looking back up at Iian.

"He thinks I was the cause of your tears," he said softly. He put a hand lightly on her shoulder and she winced. The bruises had started to fade, but the muscles would take a while still to feel better. Iian removed his hand as if he had burned her and quickly looked away. "He wants to talk to you. I must be going. Maybe you will stop by the restaurant for dinner tonight? We could continue our conversation," he said, looking back at her for an answer.

"That sounds great," Megan said.

"Good, I'll see you tonight then." He leaned over and placed a small kiss on her cheek. Megan really did like Iian and his laid-back ways. She was starting to feel more comfortable around him every time she saw him. Todd, on the other hand, made her feel like a bundle of nerves. She didn't know what to think about the anger she had seen in his face, but she felt comforted that he cared about her.

When Iian left the room, she started to look through some of the advertising ideas that they had come up with. She didn't hear Todd come back into the room but instantly knew when he stood in the doorway. Her stomach did this little nervous jump, and her skin tingled. She looked up slowly and stared into those silvery eyes.

"I'm sorry about barging in. The front door was open, and well, I suppose I'm used to coming and going around here," he said with a shrug as he walked over and sat on the couch.

"That's alright. I don't mind. I'm actually enjoying feeling like part of your family. Everyone has made me feel very welcome. Your brother said you needed to speak with me."

"Yes, well, how are you adjusting?" he said, looking a little uncomfortable. "I hope my brother doesn't bother you too much."

"No, not at all, we were discussing business. I've decided to follow through with Matt's plans for the bed-and-breakfast."

"That's great, and that's actually why I came to talk to you. As you may know, your brother and I were business partners. I took care of all the legal aspects of the business, and well, Matt trusted me to take care of this part as well," he said and picked up the file he had tossed on the couch beside him. "This is a copy of your brother's will," he said, walking over and setting it on the desk. "I know you have already talked to Matt's lawyer, but I wanted to deliver these other papers directly to you."

Megan slowly opened it. At first glance, it seemed very confusing.

"It looks complicated, but it is actually pretty simple," Todd said, moving behind her. "You know that your brother left you all his assets. Well, it's the stock he had in our business I wanted to talk to you about."

She knew from the meeting with Matt's lawyer a few days earlier that there were about twenty acres that came with the house and five cabins and other buildings. There was only the old jeep left after the accident, but it was paid for. The lawyer said that the auto insurance company was going to be cutting a check for the Porsche. Then there were the stocks he had in Jordan Shipping, as well as other holdings. There was also a property in France somewhere. It had been too much for her to take in the day she had met with the lawyer.

Megan herself had quite a bit of money left over from the inheritance her parents had left her. Thank goodness Derek had never known about it. It had been released to her when she had come of age, but she had never touched it. She had assumed she would have to pull money from it to help pay her way until she could find a job.

A stock sheet labeled Jordan Shipping sat in front of her. Megan could feel the heat from Todd's body as he leaned over and turned the pages, looking for the right one. She could smell the clean scent of his soap and it had her stomach doing little twists.

Turning to yet another page, he continued, "Let me know whether you want to liquidate any of Matt's assets. I have personal interest in the stock, but I could help you find someone to help you sell anything else." He finished speaking, but didn't move away.

Megan turned her head to thank him and realized how close he was to her. She could not only smell his soap, she could almost taste it.

He had meant to move away, really he had, but then he had smelled her hair. It smelled of violets and spring. She had her head turned down towards the file, and her neck was exposed to his view. What was his fascination with this woman's neck?

When he had walked in earlier to see her sitting in Matt's leather chair with tears in her eyes and Iian leaning over her, he'd had a flash of rage so strong he had wanted to take his brother outside and pound some sense into him.

She turned her eyes towards him. Her eyes were the color of the fields after a rain. When she let go of a small breath, he groaned. Then, when her tongue darted out to moisten her full bottom lip, he lost it. He grabbed her shoulders and pulled her up out of the chair and to her toes.

"Why are you doing this to me?" he asked, right before he crushed her lips under his. He liked to think of himself as controlled, but now he didn't care if he was losing it.

When he had pulled her closer to his chest, her left hand had gone up in defense. But when his mouth came down to hers, she let go and melted against his chest.

He played his tongue against her lips, then took advantage when she opened them, darting his tongue inside for a taste. He knew that once he got a taste of her, things would only get worse. She was spoiling him for any other and he didn't care. This was madness and he was slowly losing his grip and sinking.

He was about to push her away from him, when he heard her moan and felt her melt further against him. Just that small sound coming from deep down caused him to pull her closer, instead. He put his hand on the back of her neck, interlacing his fingers in her soft hair, and lowered his other hand to the middle of her back, flexing his fingers and bunching up the shirt she had on.

When he realized it was one of Matt's old shirts, it was like a cold bucket of water hitting him full force.

He released her at once, stumbling back. He was going mad—this was Matt's little sister. He had all but swallowed her whole and on Matt's desk, too. In

Matt's office! Matt's sister! Damn it, he had to get it together.

He shook his head and looked at Megan. She was flushed and her lips were swollen from his. She had her hand on her cheek and he could see that it was pink and heated. Her hair was messed up from his hands, and her eyes showed shock and confusion as she remained standing there like a statue.

"I won't apologize for kissing you. I've wanted to do that for a long time. But I'll apologize for not handling it more smoothly." She was still bruised, and he hadn't been as gentle as he should have. "The papers are all there. If you have any questions, call me." He turned and walked out, leaving her leaning against the desk with her hand still against her cheek.

She wasn't quite sure what he meant by a long time, since she'd only known him for a month. But she did know that she'd never been kissed like that before. She was small, but she didn't want to be handled like she would break, at least not by him.

Her lips were still vibrating. Hell, her whole body was vibrating. She sat down in the chair since she was sure her knees would give out any moment. She could still taste him and she wanted more. What was she thinking? She sat there for a few minutes, playing it over and over in her mind.

The more she thought about it, the more she was sure she wanted it to happen again. She had come here trying to start a new life and right now that meant no men. Period! End of story. No way! She couldn't trust anyone again, let alone herself around someone new. She needed to stand on her own, find out who she truly was.

But wow, what a kiss!

Part of her screamed to take pleasure where pleasure was given.

Shaking her head to clear it of Todd, she glanced back down at the paperwork and started reading from page one. Two and a half hours later, she was to the point where she thought she might hyperventilate.

There were papers scattered all over the desk. This couldn't be right. She had gone over the figures at least six times. She had her copy of Matt's will, which the lawyer had given her two days ago, along with a stack of other papers. Her hand was shaking slightly when she reached for the phone on the desk and dialed Todd's number.

"Hello?" Lacey's sultry voice came over the phone

"Hi, Lacey, it's me, Megan."

"Hi, Megan. Iian says that you're coming to dinner tonight. You'll love it. He's going to make a special treat just for the occasion. Todd told me he dropped off the paperwork today. Were you calling because you had some questions?"

"Yes," Megan began. "Actually, quite a few. Is Todd there by any chance?"

"Hang on a minute. He's out feeding the horses. Let me ring him in the barn." Megan could hear another dial tone, then more ringing. Todd's voice came over the line. "Yeah, what's up?"

"Hey, Todd, Megan had some questions about the papers. See you tonight, Megan." There was a click before Megan had time to answer back.

"Um, hi. I had a few questions about some of these figures," Megan began. She felt awkward, but wanted to clear up any confusion she had.

"Well, how about I finish up with the horses and come over? Then we can head over to the restaurant together for dinner. Iian says that you were going over there, tonight."

"Yes, that sounds fine, thank you." Megan felt like a teenager making her first date.

"I'll see you in about an hour, then."

When Megan hung up the phone, she felt her cheeks turning pink all over again. As she went upstairs to change, she passed the mirror hanging over the coat rack by the door. Not only were her cheeks pink, her eyes sparkled. She had to stop this. What power did Todd possess to make her body react this way?

Think, Megan! She told herself. New life, no man, new life, no man. She chanted it to herself as she jogged up the stairs. An hour didn't give her a lot of time to get ready. With her broken arm, things took double the time.

By the time she heard Todd's car drive up, she was as ready as she would ever be. She had just walked out of the bedroom when she heard the front door open. She heard a small curse and it closed again. She had reached the top of the stairs when she heard the knock. She chuckled. He really was used to walking right in. They all seemed very comfortable around the house, moving as if it was second nature to them. It was kind of weird to think about how Matt had intertwined himself with their family. Then again, Matt had been a very comfortable person. She knew that once you were in with Matt, you were in for life.

Megan opened the door to see Todd's back, and what a back it was! He had changed from his jeans and work shirt to dark gray dress pants and a black blazer. She couldn't see whether he wore a tie or not but couldn't imagine him wearing one.

He turned and she forgot all about her chant of new life, no man.

She looked good enough to devour. She had changed from her jeans and Matt's old shirt to simple black dress pants that looked like they floated on the air and a light green button-up blouse. The sleeves were short enough for a small amount of arm to show above her cast.

"Come in. You know, you don't have to knock. I think I'm getting used to your family coming and going around this house," she said with a smile.

She smiled at him and he silently cursed himself. No matter what she said, he couldn't just walk in like he had when Matt was around.

"You look very lovely." Had his voice just cracked? Man, here he was almost thirty-two years old, and he felt like he was on his first date again. He cleared his throat. They stood there for a minute taking each other in. "You had some questions about the paperwork?"

"Oh, yes." She moved back into the office, her heels clicking on the hardwood floors, and then sat down behind the oak desk. "Here, where I have it marked, the total of liquid assets. This can't be right." Todd moved over to look. The number on the paper was correct; Todd had seen to it himself. "Also, here where it shows the working capital total?"

"I assure you, these numbers are correct," he said looking down at the paper.

"But then, um, that would mean…" Megan couldn't finish.

"Your brother was well versed in his financial options. Jordan Shipping stock was, and is, a solid investment. You don't need to worry about anything. Your brother made sure you would be taken care of after he was gone." Todd stepped back. If he didn't, he might not want to back off at all.

"But how did he invest in so much stock? I mean…" She was stuttering and starting to feel foolish. "It's just that my brother never seemed to have any money when I was growing up. How did he…?" She couldn't finish.

"From what he mentioned, he had taken his inheritance and invested years ago, and when that investment paid off, he invested again. When he moved here, he paid cash for the land and house. About a year later he invested in Jordan Shipping, which, if I do say so myself, has paid off quite nicely over the last four years. Your brother purchased enough stock in our company that I asked him to be on the board, and then two years ago, I made him a full partner. He was a good asset to the business. He was not only a brilliant man but also my mentor. I looked up to him quite a lot. My entire family did."

She listened to him talk about her brother and wondered whether she really had known the man. The Matt she knew always had money in his pockets, never in the bank. When she had lived with him, she had questioned whether he had even owned the clothes on his back. He was very laid back, never took anything too seriously, and almost always had his nose in a book.

He was a traveler, a wanderer, never really stopping in one place for long. He had always provided an apartment or condo for them to live in, but Megan was uprooted almost every year. And after she had gone off to live at the college dorm, things had moved even faster for Matt, or so she had thought.

She knew he had moved here almost five years ago, right after she married, but even then, he had traveled a lot. Not once had she thought that he was investing his inheritance. She had paid off her college tuition and put a down payment on the townhouse she had lived in when she had married. But after that, she hadn't really touched it for fear that Derek would find it.

She couldn't get her mind around it. According to these documents, everything was taken care of—the house, the land, the vehicles—and there was enough money to make the bed-and-breakfast a huge success. His stock accounts covered all of it, and so much more.

Matt's holdings amounted to enough that she wouldn't have to worry about anything for the remainder of her life. Why hadn't her brother told her? Had he guessed about Derek? Is that why he had kept all this from her?

Chapter Five

Todd could see the color leaving her face, so he tried to interrupted her thoughts. "Are you hungry?"

She looked up at him and blinked. "What?" she asked in a shaky voice.

"Are you hungry?" he repeated as he took her hand in his and pulled her up from the chair, setting her on her feet. "Shall we go have some of the best food around?"

The short drive to the restaurant was pleasant. As he drove, Todd talked about the town and the people, trying to prevent her from thinking about the papers back on the desk. He was sure it would only take some time for her to adjust to it. This would give her a chance at a new life, but it had cost her the most important person in her life. What a price to pay!

They drove up to the restaurant, a huge building that sat right on the waterfront. Large white lanterns lit up the whole front of the building. The older two-story building had new, whitewashed siding. A decorative hand-carved sign hung over the front doors. *The Golden Oar* was carved in vibrant gold letters above a ship with white sails, which sat in dark blue waters. Lacey looked enchanted.

Todd parked the car and helped her out. Her eyes were fixed on the building in front of them.

"It's been recently remodeled," he said, taking her left elbow and walking them towards the door.

"This is really Iian and Lacey's baby. That's mine over there," he said, pointing to a four-story brick building across the way. "Jordan Shipping" was in big white letters across the top. "We'll save that tour for another day," he said, guiding her towards the restaurant.

He would always think of himself as a sailor. But the truth of it was, since his father's death almost four years ago, he's spent more time behind a desk than behind the wheel of a ship..

"Iian runs the kitchen here and Lacey runs everything else, including Iian," he said with a smile. "I mainly stay out of their way." They walked through double doors that had "Welcome to the Golden Oar" etched in the glass.

Instantly, Todd's senses were flooded with a hundred memories of family, friends, and his youth. The place was packed as always on Friday nights.

Lacey was greeted by a rush of warmth. She found the smells and sounds of the fine family restaurant to be soothing. The lighting was soft and warm, and the walls were covered with elegant oil paintings. A huge stone fireplace sat near the back of the room. There was a wall made of glass that overlooked the water, giving the guests a sense of romance and elegance.

A high-school-aged employee dressed in a red and white sailor shirt with a name tag that said Britney greeted them at the door. "Good evening, Mr. Jordan. Table for two?"

"Better make it for four. If I know my brother and sister, they'll be along shortly."

And sure enough, as Britney was seating them, Lacey walked over carrying a tray over her shoulder with glasses and dishes on it. She wore her usual red and white striped shirt but instead of slacks, she wore a short black skirt with black hose and flats.

"Hi guys, give me a minute and I'll be right back," she said, and then hurried off towards another table.

"Usually, she only waits tables on Friday nights. That's when we're the busiest," Todd explained as he pulled out the chair for her.

"Thank you. Wow! What a view," she said, looking out the windows next to their table.

The sun was setting, lighting up the sky with hues of pink and purples. The lights from the boats along the shore glowed and gleamed in the fading day light.

"During the day, you can see clear up the coast," he said, handing her a menu. "At least on a clear day."

The table was set with low candles, a small vase of white flowers, cloth napkins, and paper place mats. It felt right. It was a warm mix of family and romance that gave the place character. Fishing nets and oars hung on the walls, but what really caught her eye were the paintings.

Colorful oil paintings depicted scenes of violent, stormy oceans, colorful sunsets over calm waters, and boats filled with fishermen. Some paintings had underwater cities with merpeople swimming in the background.

Above the stone fireplace was a painting of a mermaid who had green eyes so like her own, she had to blink.

The mermaid was poised as if she were daydreaming, staring off to some distant place. She ran a shell comb through the long blonde tresses that covered most of her chest. Her tail was a vibrant green that seemed to sparkle when Megan turned her head from side to side.

"The first time I saw you, I thought of her," Todd said, noticing her survey of the mermaid. "You have your brother's eyes, but you also have hers," he said, nodding towards the picture. "My great-grandmother was the artist of everything hanging in here. She was a little eccentric, but my great-grandfather always helped to keep her feet on the shore. Some say that she came from the sea, rather than Southern California," he said with a wicked grin.

"They're wonderful. I've always wanted to have a talent like painting, but both Matt and I have two left hands when it comes to art. Did any of the talent survive the generations?" Megan asked, looking down at her menu. On the front cover was a sketch done in the same hand as the sample advertising for the bed-and-breakfast she'd seen in the file sitting on Matt's desk. The menu's drawing was the view of the restaurant from the water. Taking a closer look at it, she saw the name in the bottom left corner and looked up at Todd.

"Yeah, I have some talent in sketching." He smiled.

"You did this? And the one for the bed-and-breakfast?" she asked, running her hands over the slick menu cover.

He smiled back. He had a great smile; his whole face lit up. She got that familiar flutter in her stomach and turned back to the menu.

"When I was seventeen, my father asked me to do some sketches. A week after drawing this one, he had the menus printed up, and they've stuck ever since. That didn't take long," he said, looking up and over her shoulder.

Megan glanced over and saw Iian making his way over to their table. He had long strides and walked as if he had a purpose. Sitting in a chair next to her, he started signing something to Todd. Why did it appear to her that the brothers were always competing for attention?

"You'll excuse me for a few minutes. It appears there's a matter in the back I need to deal with," Todd said, setting his napkin on the table. He headed out the double doors that led back to the kitchen.

Iian leaned in, taking her hand, and whispered to her, "You look lovely tonight." Megan felt a warm feeling spread up her hand where he was holding it. Then the light went on in her head. They *were* in competition—for her. She suddenly lost the ability to think, speak, and breathe. What would she say? What could she say?

"I'm glad you came tonight," he said, right before Lacey walked up with a bottle of red wine and four glasses. She sat down and rubbed her hands together.

"Wow, busy tonight. Have you had a chance to look over the menu yet?" she asked, pouring the wine.

"No, I'm sorry. But since I have the chef here"—she looked over at Iian—"what do you suggest?" She reached out and took a sip of the wine. It went down smooth and started to calm her nerves.

Iian smiled and signed the order to Lacey. Lacey smiled back and said to Megan, "Oh, you'll love it," then she jumped up and rushed off to place the order.

Luckily, right then Todd came back and sat down, signing something to his brother. Megan was really going to need to study up on sign language; she felt left out of half the conversations. Then again, she supposed they weren't used to having outsiders sit in on all of their conversations. She imagined it was kind of like eavesdropping.

From there on, she was saved from fending off any more advances from Iian as the conversation flowed from local events and places to ideas about the bed-and-breakfast. Megan split her attention between the two brothers.

The wine was relaxing her, and she enjoyed seeing the brothers interact with each other when they weren't competing for her attention. They appeared to enjoy each other's company, sometimes laughing at stories they told about their youth.

She enjoyed the night immensely, and the meal was the best she'd eaten in a long time. They'd had smoked salmon with a wine sauce and sweet vegetables. Lacey had been popping in to the table and grabbing a bite off of Todd or Iian's plates when time allowed.

Iian was an excellent chef, and she joked about how he could have prepared the food when he'd not once left their table. He joked back about having little elves that did his bidding.

"He's just being modest. All the recipes are either handed down from our ancestors, or created by Iian himself, like the meal we enjoyed tonight," Todd said, smiling over at his brother.

"It was good," Megan signed. She had picked up a few signs during their conversations. Todd signed when he spoke to his brother, probably out of habit, but she didn't mind; she enjoyed seeing their hands move.

“Thank you,” Iian signed back and gave her a grin. “I’d better get back before those elves start making shoes instead of food. I enjoyed your company tonight, Megan,” he said, leaning over her hand and kissing her knuckles. His lips were warm and soft and she smiled back up at him.

She only flinched slightly at his touch, a definite improvement.

“I think he likes you,” Todd said, pouring more wine in her glass after Iian had disappeared into the back.

Megan fumbled with her wine glass, almost spilling it. She was at a loss for words.

“Don’t worry, he likes all women. If you want to learn more about sign language,” he said, quickly changing the subject, “I can help. Iian only talks around you. Talking really does make him uncomfortable. For the first two years after his accident, he didn’t speak a word.”

“What happened?” Megan asked, taking another sip of her wine.

“He and Dad had gone on a weeklong fishing trip in the sailboat. This was over four years ago when Iian had just turned eighteen. Dad called it his “becoming a man” voyage. All we know is that when they found Iian in the raft, he was unconscious and seriously dehydrated, and he had a bad case of hypothermia, a concussion, and a couple broken ribs. Dad and the boat were never found. Iian can only remember bits and pieces about what happened, but nothing about the accident itself. We estimated that he had been in the water for almost ten hours before we found him."

"I'm so sorry." Megan reached out and took his hand. "I lost both of my parents when I was young." Looking down at their joined hands, she noticed how large his were compared to her own.

"Matt told me that they had died when you were young. We had a hard time dealing with Dad's death. Then we had to learn a new language to communicate with each other, and somehow we grew closer. Matt had moved to Pride a year earlier. Lacey had met him in Paris when she lived there for a while. When he moved here, he fit right into the family. He was instrumental in helping me recover and take over my father's business. Your brother was a great man. I think continuing with his dream for the bed-and-breakfast is a great idea." He squeezed her hand slightly.

"He would be very proud of you. He was always proud of you, but this was something he'd dreamed you would want to be a part of. Ever since he first came up with the idea, he wanted you to move here, you know."

"I—he hadn't mentioned it to me. I had some… issues to deal with on my own." She pulled her hand back and folded them in her lap, feeling the guilt spread again.

In truth, after the divorce, she'd needed to feel like she could make it on her own. Then, after the disaster last month, she'd made up her mind to move to Oregon, to move in with her brother. But she had wanted to wait until she'd healed before letting her brother see her. Now she would do anything to change that decision.

"I should have been here," she said more to herself than to Todd.

"You couldn't have changed anything. And you could have both been in the car that night when the trucker lost control." He was right, she knew it, yet that didn't stop the guilt.

"Let's go take a walk." He stood and helped her put on her coat.

It was a chilly night, but it hadn't rained that afternoon, so it was warmer than the other nights. As they walked out onto the pier, she took a deep breath. She could smell the salt water and the food from the restaurant. The night was clear, and they could see all the stars in the sky. She pulled her jacket closer to her. It was hard since she was unable to put her right arm through the sleeves, so she left it tucked up close to her body. She couldn't wait until the cast came off.

Lacey shivered when they walked out, so Todd pulled her closer and put his arm around her shoulders lightly. “How’s the back?” he asked in an easy tone.

“Oh, much better. That stuff you gave me really does help. I think I’ve gone from purple to green in record time.” She blushed and turned her face towards the sea.

Putting his fingers under her chin, he brought her face back to his. “Megan, you can talk to me. I won’t judge and I won’t hurt you.”

“I know. Your whole family has been so good to me. I—I’m not ready. I want to start my new life and forget the past. Can you understand?” she said, looking up into his eyes.

“I’m here if you decide you need to talk. We all are. You may think that you’re alone, but you don’t have to be.” He ran his finger lightly down the side of her neck. Pulling her closer, he felt her shiver again, this time not from the wind.

Her life had been a circus the last couple weeks. She could tell herself she didn’t need anyone now, but the fact was, being held had never felt so good.

Being a part of his family had opened something she'd long ago closed up and forgotten.

Todd was warm. She could feel the heat radiating from him, which caused her to shiver again. He pulled her close. Her encased arm was tucked between their bodies and she could feel his stomach muscles bunch and flex against her hand. Then he pulled back and looked down at her. Her eyes darted once to his mouth, which instantly rose up on one side in a small smile. His mouth was very potent. She remembered the heat his lips had branded her with earlier that day.

"I feel something for you, Megan. I don't know what it is yet, but it's there." He lowered his head towards hers.

The kiss was soft, warming her to the toes. She put her free arm around him, wishing that her other one was free to do the same. She thought that it would be like the first kiss, but this time, it was slower, more intense. She started shaking again.

"Let me come home with you," he said softly into her hair, minutes later.

She could imagine it, the two of them intertwined. Hadn't she dreamed about it since their first meeting? What would it be like to take a casual lover? Could she afford to allow him in? Could she trust him, and more importantly, could she trust herself?

"No." It slipped from her lips. The one word stopped him; she knew the fear was written in her eyes this time. Pulling his head back, he took in her whole face. Her shoulders were tensed and she pulled away. This time he let her go.

"I can't do this Todd, not now." She leaned against the railing, once again raising her eyes towards the dark skies. "I'm a wreck. I just want to pull myself together. I can't get involved now. Can you understand?"

He walked over and leaned his hip against the railing next to her, looking into her face instead of the ocean. "I'm not in any hurry." She jerked her head around to face him. When he continued to stare at her, she turned back around to face the ocean. They stood there, she looking out over the dark water and he looking at her, in silence for a while.

Iian had watched them leave. He knew his brother had a hard time when it came to relationships. It had only been five years since Sara had died along with their unborn baby girl. His brother hadn't even gone out on a date since then. There was something special about Megan, and the whole Jordan clan knew it. It was more than her fitting in; she was part of the family, already.

When he'd seen her in the muddy graveyard, broken and crying, he had wanted to pick her up and comfort her as a brother would. But he knew Todd had other feelings for her; he'd seen it that first night in the living room. He knew his brother a little better after losing his hearing. After all, some of his senses had become sharper. But one thing was clear; Todd had already lost his heart to Megan. Now he only needed to help Megan find hers.

The house was filled with lights when Todd arrived back home after dropping Megan off. He enjoyed living with his brother and sister sometimes, but tonight he wished for some time alone. So instead of walking back to the house, he turned and walked to the barn to check on Chester.

Chester was a black shire horse. He was a great big beast he had fallen in love with at first sight. He'd gotten him years ago to help work the fields. Of course, he had also purchased a John Deere that year as well. But Chester was his connection to the old ways. He enjoyed riding the gentle giant through the fields, taking the time to groom him and care for him. Chester played a huge part in Todd's stress relief.

As Todd walked into the barn, Chester gave him a snort of acknowledgment. "Good evening. How's my big boy?" he walked over to the stall and gave Chester a carrot. "I'll let you in on a secret," Todd said, leaning on Chester's neck while patting him. "I think I'm in big trouble, and I just might like it."

Chapter Six

"A hot tub?" Megan's head began to swim.

She'd gone to the local hardware and lumber store to pick up some paint and supplies she needed to start work on the cabins. While she was there, the owner, a Mr. Kent, had informed her that Matt had ordered several larger items and that they would be in next week. He had been instructed to deliver and setup these items. When Megan asked what supplies they were, Mr. Kent smiled.

"Well, it's that tub he ordered last month. He wanted to put it on that new deck he built off his bedroom. He spent all last summer building that thing with the Jordan boys; it turned out pretty nice. He also ordered a couple of small refrigerators, fancy bath tubs, and sinks for those other two cabins of his, real expensive ones, too. They're supposed to be in on Tuesday. I'll give you a call when they come in, and we could start installing them the next day if you want." She had known about the other appliances, having seen the receipts in her file. But she hadn't known about the hot tub. Then it hit her. Next week! This wouldn't give her a lot of time to get everything done.

Twenty minutes later, she was leaving the hardware store with the help of two young employees. The young high school boys helped her put the items into the Jeep and quickly ran back into the store. Her vehicle was now weighed down with paint, a paint sprayer, some tarps, stain, and some tools she thought she would need.

She took a look around the small town. Every time she came into town, she found more reasons to like it. People were walking around Main Street. There was a small barbershop, and three older men sat out front smoking. It reminded her of a picture she'd seen on a calendar once.

Across the street was a quaint little antique store with a small sign that read "Adams' Antiques" hanging above the door.

Megan headed for it. She'd been enjoying the quiet and seclusion of the house, but her new life wouldn't really start until she made herself part of this town, and she was determined to make her new life here work.

The townspeople seemed very open and welcoming to her. People waved or said, "Hi," when she walked by. Maybe it was because Matt had made a good impression, but she could do her part to fit in.

A bell chimed as she walked through the door of the shop. A young woman was sitting behind the counter. She had a paintbrush in one hand and a phone in the other. Nodding "hello" towards her, Megan started walking around the small store. She immediately found items she wanted for the cabins. There were small statues, some of children dancing in a circle around a fire, one of a lone wolf howling up at a moon. Megan noticed some brass candlesticks and an oak coat rack. She picked out a small writing desk, a couple of benches, and some other items that she wanted.

"If you need any help let me know," the woman said after hanging up the phone. "You're Matt's sister, Megan, right?" When Megan nodded, the woman continued. "I'm Allison Adams. I knew your brother. He was a good man." She stepped out from behind the counter with the paintbrush still in hand. She wore a white apron covered in paint over her blouse and jeans. She was probably six foot tall and had medium honey hair that was shoulder length. She had a figure that came straight off of a magazine cover.

"Thank you. Your store is lovely," Megan said, feeling small and plain. "I'm interested in this statue here, those candlesticks, this coat rack, and do you happen to have another coat rack like this one?" She looked around and noticed some other items she pointed out to Allison.

"Fixing up the cabins?" When Megan nodded again, she said, "That's good. I have another coat rack in the back. It isn't oak though, it's maple," she said, walking to a back room.

Megan walked into a small room and noticed several paintings leaning against the walls "Are these yours?" Megan asked, stepping in and looking around.

"It's a hobby of mine. Keeps me busy during the slow hours." Noticing Megan's interest, she continued. "Would you like to see them?" she asked, motioning Megan further into the room.

"I'd love to." There were paintings as big as a wall, and ones that could fit in the palm of her hands. There was artwork in oil, watercolor, chalk, and pencil. Their topics ranged from fairytale creatures to local buildings and people. There was also a charcoal of the town. The oils were in dark, rich colors. They were all top quality and beautifully done, most of them more beautifully done than the ones Megan had seen at the Golden Oar.

"You did all of these?" Megan asked while walking around. She saw a charcoal of the three men sitting outside the barbershop next door and let out a laugh.

"Yeah, well there are a lot of slow hours around here," Allison said with a half smile.

She found several paintings that would go great in the cabins and one she wanted in her bedroom. She really liked the pixies and small winged creatures that completely covered one huge canvas.

"Do you…would you sell any of these?" Megan asked, looking over her shoulder.

"Well, I've never sold any before," she said, chewing her bottom lip. "Well, except to my mother, of course. I guess I could part with some. Which ones are you interested in?"

Megan took her time setting paintings aside. She had picked out the wall of pixies and a couple small watercolors of a pack of wolves running in front of a full moon. She also picked an oil painting of the bay, a charcoal of the town, the one of the old men, and six other oil paintings.

"All of these?" Allison asked, sounding a little winded.

"Yes, I love these. I must have them. Do you happen to know where I can buy frames?" Megan asked, trying to not sound too eager.

"I can order frames for you. I have a book we can look through and pick them out," she said, walking back to the front of the store.

For the next hour, the two women leaned over a book of frames. They picked a frame out for each picture she had purchased. Megan found she liked picking out these little details for the cabins. It made her feel that she was really starting to find herself. When they had picked out the last frame, she looked up into Allison's sparkling eyes and something hit her. She not only was feeling really good about herself, she'd made Allison feel good about herself as well. Maybe she wasn't the only person in town who needed another chance.

"You know, I bet that if you had the other paintings framed, you could sell them here in your store," Megan said.

"Well, no one has been interested in my stuff before," Allison said, chewing her bottom lip again.

"I bet you would sell them like crazy if you could get them in art galleries in Portland. City tourists go crazy about local artists. I actually know someone who owns a gallery in Portland and Seattle."

"Oh, thank you, that's very kind, but…well…I don't think my art is good enough for a gallery and well…" Her statement dropped away.

"Nonsense, it's better than a lot of that stuffy art I've seen in a lot of galleries. I bet you anything your art sells faster than…well…anything," Megan said, smiling over the counter at Allison.

Allison's whole face lit up. "You really think other people would buy it?"

"I've been in the marketing business for years. I know when I find something that would be easy to sell. You have a lot of talent. I think people would love your art. I know I do," she said smiling. "And I was thinking about the possibility of commissioning you to do a couple more, an oil painting of each of my cabins. That is, after I have finished the landscape work and repairs. I would also like to have one done of the main house. You can have business cards printed and place them in the corner of each painting I hang up so that my customers will know about your store."

"You really are like your brother, aren't you?" Allison said, leaning back in her chair.

With all the items that Megan had purchased, including a dozen of her paintings and frames, Allison claimed to have the biggest sales day she had ever had.

An hour later, Allison helped Megan carry the smaller items to her rental car with a promise of delivering the larger ones on Friday, and all the paintings after the frames had been delivered.

The next morning, Megan was out putting bird food in the new feeder she'd purchased when she heard a lawn mower start up in the front yard. After jumping almost a foot at the sound, she calmed down and dusted herself off and then walked around the house cautiously. Everywhere around the yard, she could see green starting to poke up from the flowerbeds. The weather was getting warmer, and spring was almost here. Reaching the front yard, she noticed Iian pushing an older model mower around the grass. It appeared that he was comfortable doing the job and the grass really did need mowing. Forcing herself to relax, she ran in and made him some iced tea.

After making the instant tea, she brought a pitcher and two glasses to the covered porch and sat down until he was finished with the front yard.

When the mower stopped, she poured them both a glass. Iian waved and walked over, sitting down next to her. He drank his tea down in two gulps. His white shirt was sticking to his chest, and what a chest it was. A woman would have to be blind not to appreciate a body like his.

He set his glass down and signed slowly with each word. "I figured you would need some help with the yard work until your arm is healed."

"Thank you. I can get my cast removed next week, so I should be able to start doing more myself," she said.

"That's good. I broke my leg when I was ten. Todd helped me use a saw to cut off the cast a few weeks later. I couldn't stand having it on; it itched like crazy."

"Yes, I've almost removed this one myself a few times." Iian chuckled at her face. She had it bunched up in a sour look.

"I'm sure I could find an old saw in the garage," he joked.

"No, I don't think I would trust you or your brother with a saw." At this, Iian exploded in laughter.

They sat and talked for another half hour, and then Iian finished mowing the backyard and left. She was picking up sign language quickly and enjoyed learning it. He always made a point to help her learn simple words. Being able to only use her good hand didn't help her learn, but she could do most of the simple words and she muddled through the rest.

Once she made up her mind to finish the cabins, it seemed to her that her ear was stuck to the phone, with calls to and from electricians, plumbers, and everyone else. Time went by quickly and before she knew it, the contractor trucks were parked in her driveway and there were men hauling stuff out to the cabins.

On the first morning, it was almost eleven before she was able to have her first cup of coffee. She'd been running back and forth, opening the cabins and showing the contractors around. She was on edge and almost ready to call it quits. Then the coffee had worked into her bloodstream and all seemed right again. The rest of the day went off without a hitch.

Even when Father Michael stopped by, she dealt with his visit with grace and patience. He seemed somewhat overly protective of her and she enjoyed it. He had of course visited on several occasions before. She'd even had several visits from the churchwomen, as Lacey called them. There was a group of them, all silver haired, frail looking and very overwhelming. She enjoyed their visits, but enjoyed it more after they left and the house was quiet again.

It seemed that every day there was a Jordan in her house, bringing or making food. They even helped her on several occasions with the cabins. She enjoyed feeling like part of their family and truly felt blessed. She looked forward to their daily visits.

The next few days were filled with contractors coming and going. The work was a long, slow process for her, but she managed with Todd and Iian's help to start painting the last cabin herself with the sprayer she'd purchased.

They had shown up one day and helped her prepare and tape all the rooms for painting. She had rented a sander for the floors, and Iian had taken to it like it was the coolest toy he'd ever seen. Before she could even blink, he had the remaining two cabin floors sanded and ready to stain. She had really wanted to try the sanding machine out herself, but she couldn't complain about the help. Every time Iian came, he brought wonderful sandwiches and soup for all the workers, which of course, put everyone in a better working mood.

Iian brought over food one afternoon after a hard morning of work. They sat on the front porch eating at her small table and talking about what she should plant in her garden, when an old blue truck drove up and parked in the drive.

Megan was excited to see Allison step out and wave up to them. Allison had on a white dress that flowed when she walked, making her look even taller than before. "I've got your paintings here," she called up.

"Oh! Good!" Megan hopped up and started down the stairs, when she realized Iian was still sitting on the chair. He was looking at Allison with a funny look on his face, and his whole body was tense. Megan turned back to him. "You know Allison Adams? She brought the paintings I bought from her. Can you help us get them from the truck?" she asked.

He nodded and followed her down the stairs.

"Hi, Iian." Allison paused from pulling out one of the larger paintings. She had jumped into the bed of the truck and was handing the paintings down.

Iian nodded. Megan thought it was strange how he was acting, but then she noticed all the pictures wrapped with brown paper, and she forgot about it.

"Oh, the frames came in. Wow. That was fast." She began ripping off the paper on the one she held. "Oh, they look so professional," Megan said, holding it up. Iian looked over her shoulder at the painting, noticing the small signature in the corner, and then looked back up at Allison with shock registering on his face.

"I really like the look of this small one that you had matted and framed," Allison said, holding it up and walking to the back of the truck. Iian quickly walked over and helped her down from the bed of the truck. When Megan noticed that his hands stayed on Allison's hips a little longer than necessary, she quickly looked away, smiling to herself.

"You did these?" Iian asked in a quiet voice.

Allison nodded and visibly blushed, then went back to moving the paintings to the edge of the truck. Iian had his hands shoved into his pockets and was staring at a rock by his foot.

When all the art was moved safely into the house and unwrapped, she asked, "Would you like to stay for lunch? Iian has enough food to feed a small army."

"Oh, well, I don't want to interrupt your lunch…" Allison broke off, looking back and forth between Iian and Megan.

Megan noticed the quick looks and almost laughed. Realizing that her back was to Iian, she quickly assured Allison that Iian was only a good friend. When Allison took a quick step back towards the door, she realized that the girl was scared and very nervous. "I would really enjoy the company."

"Oh, well, I guess." Allison's voice dropped off as she looked over at Iian again.

"Good," Megan interrupted. "Come on, we were just eating out on the front porch."

Iian no longer talked out loud. Instead, he would sign to Megan slowly enough for her to understand. She had learned the alphabet and basic words enough to get along.

"This chicken is very good," Allison said to Iian. He nodded in reply and smiled slightly, handing her a roll.

Todd had mentioned that Iian only talked around people he felt comfortable around. He looked very uncomfortable now and within five minutes of finishing his plate, he was back up and signing that he had to go to work. Then he left quickly and quietly.

Allison stayed for another hour, helping Megan hang some of the pictures in the house. The ones for the cabins would have to be hung after she was done painting.

She enjoyed Allison's company, and she told Allison that her friend who owned the gallery, Ric Derby, was interested in seeing some of her paintings. She had called him right after her first visit with Allison. He'd been excited to know that Megan had moved to the west coast and was looking forward to her visit. It had seemed to her that he'd been more interested in seeing her than Allison's paintings, but she didn't pass that information on to Allison. Allison said she was excited about having a professional's opinion of her art.

After Allison left for the evening, Megan took a walk. She enjoyed the cool evenings, and there was a footpath that she'd discovered not too long ago that led to a small pond. The pond sat at the corner of her property where it joined with the Jordan's property and the property of her other neighbors, the Bells.

She enjoyed her walks to the beach, but the pond was closer, and she found it more soothing. Tonight the water was quiet and surreal. She'd taken several walks there, sometimes taking along a book to read as she sat on a big flat rock by the water. Fat frogs jumped around the water's edge, and once, Megan had seen a deer drinking on the other side of the pond.

She could just imagine this place as magical. She thought the dragonflies could turn into small fairies, like in Allison's paintings, when no one was looking. The frogs could turn into princes, who would spend their days lying around the pond, lazily enjoying the water.

Currently, it was almost too dark to see any frogs or dragonflies. The sun had yet to go down, but the trees sheltered the trail from the sun's light. Megan had grabbed the flashlight and one of Matt's old jackets, knowing that it would be dark before she returned to the house. She felt safe in this place, peaceful. It had been a long time since she'd felt like doing nothing. Her life had been pretty busy in the city. She'd always been on the go, running errands, working, or just hiding from Derek.

Now, as she took her place on the rock to overlook the water, she imagined life like this years from now. Would she be sitting here by herself? Did she want to be sitting here by herself? She knew she wasn't quite ready for a relationship. She knew it would take a lot for her to be able to trust someone, especially a man. But she didn't want to live life not having faith in the good of mankind.

Sure, she had a rough past, and her luck with men was terrible. But looking back on Matt's life gave her some hope. Men like Matt did exist and she'd known a few other good people in her life.

Her old boss, Mr. Martin, was one of them. He had always been very kind to her. Ric Derby, the owner of the Blue Spot Galleries, an account she had worked on in the past, had been wonderful to her also.

Iian was another one. He was always a fun conversationalist and she never felt scared around him. He always went out of his way to make her smile. She enjoyed that he flirted with her; it had been a long time since she had felt attractive. Even though he was a few years younger than she was, Megan enjoyed the attention.

And then there was Todd. She couldn't quite get a handle on him. She was desperately attracted to him and that scared her. He made her feel like a bundle of nerves, but he was kind and showed her gentleness that she'd never seen in a man. The way he had rubbed her back that night had given her things to dream about, and dream about them she had.

Her last dream had been so real, she'd woken up still feeling his hands on her. Smiling to herself, she replayed it in her mind.

It had started out with her sitting on the front porch, swinging on the swing. Todd had ridden across the field on a huge black horse. Saying nothing, he dismounted in one fluid motion, walked up the stairs and pulled her up into his arms. Then he carried her into the house and gently laid her down on a soft bed covered with pink rose petals. His lips branding her, his hands had parted the white dress she was wearing and then they wreaked havoc on her skin, causing her body to bow and heat.

When he'd bent his head to kiss her breast, she had woken. Her skin had tingled and her nipples were hardened, waiting for the wet feel of his mouth. She'd been so sure that she could still feel his hands on her, she'd reached up and touched just there.

Then Megan heard a loud snort, and her eyes darted up. There across the pond sat Todd on the biggest black horse she'd ever seen. It was like they'd just stepped out of her dream. Megan blinked a few times to make sure the image didn't disappear on her. He sat bareback on the beast and looked like the romantic figure her dream had created.

When they started walking around the pond towards her, she quickly got up off her perch and dusted her pants off. Her heart was still racing from remembering her dream, and she felt flushed. Her hands were shaking, and she was not quite sure what to do with them, so she shoved them deep into the pockets of Matt's old jacket.

"Good evening, Megan," Todd said, jumping down from the horse. His movements were fluid and she could see his muscles flex under his light T-shirt when he reached and pulled the reins over the horse's head.

"Hi," she said. "Who is this enchanting creature?" she asked walking over to the beast.

"He's very friendly," he said when he saw her reach her hand out then quickly pull it back when Chester let out a soft snort.

Todd reached down and, putting her hand in his, pulled them up to Chester's mane together.

Chester let out a soft breath and then nuzzled Megan's shoulder.

"Oh, he's such a nice, handsome gentleman." She laughed when Chester nibbled at her pockets.

"He thinks you have sugar cubes." Todd pulled two from his pocket and transferred them to her hand. "Keep your hand flat like this," he said, holding her hand in his while the beast licked her fingers clean. She smiled up at Todd. His head was bent towards hers, his eyes laughing, and her breath caught.

He bent his head down and was a breath away when Chester pushed against her shoulder again. He quickly caught her as she fell into his arms, laughing. "I think he wants more," she murmured.

"Mmm, my turn," Todd said, just before he claimed her lips in a soft kiss.

Chester let out a low nicker and then started grazing on the sweet grass nearby.

He kept the kiss soft until she let out the smallest of moans and wrapped her arm around him. Then he dragged her closer and plundered her lips.

Their tongues began dueling a battle they both enjoyed. His hands had been on her hips, but now they started to roam her small frame. He reached under her jacket with shaking hands and cupped her as his other hand pressed her closer.

Megan was back in her dream, the smells and tastes coming back to her. His hands just there and his mouth hot on hers. When he reached down to unbutton the first few buttons of the jacket, she pulled her head back, giving him access.

His lips left her mouth to trail down her neck, slowly descending towards his destination. He pulled the buttons loose on her shirt and opened the neckline to expose the white skin underneath. She wore nothing underneath tonight, and when he saw her, he groaned.

He pulled back and looked at her. "You look so beautiful," he whispered. He had pushed the jacket off her and it pooled at her feet, exposing her skin to him. He bent his head and claimed her with his lips.

His mouth was warm and set off sparks on her cooled skin. He reached over and played lightly with her other nipple, which hardened instantly. When he pulled her down to the soft grass, she went willingly.

She could smell the sweet grass as they crushed it underneath them. She felt his lips roaming over her and enjoyed the feel of him tugging lightly on her nipples.

She arched her back so he would have better access and gripped his shoulder tightly. She moved her cast arm further out of the way so it was lying on the grass beside her.

Todd's weight pinned her to the grass as he enjoyed her skin, causing goose bumps on the exposed skin. His hips were pressed up against hers, and she felt his hardness against her hip. She rubbed her hip over him and he let out a moan.

Pulling his head back, he looked down at her face.

"Megan," he began, but then Chester stuck his nose between them. Megan let out a laugh and turned her face away from the wet sloppy kisses Chester was placing on her forehead.

Laughing, Todd pushed Chester away. "Go get your own filly, this one's taken." The horse let out another snort and continued his search for sugar cubes by pushing his head in between the pair again.

Todd rolled up, pulling Megan with him, putting his body in front of Chester. Megan quickly pulled her shirt back together and avoided Todd's eyes.

"Megan, I'm sorry," he began. He bent down and picked up the jacket, brushing it off and handing it to her.

She stared back at him. "Oh, no, I mean, I'm not sorry for that," he said quickly. "I'm sorry about being rough with you. I shouldn't have pushed you to the ground…For Christ's sake, I almost took you in the dirt." He ran his hands over his face and walked back and forth in front of her.

"I'm not so fragile, Todd," Megan said quietly.

"You are and you deserve better than that." She watched him pacing and felt relieved knowing that he wanted her so much that time and place didn't matter.

"I'm not sorry. In fact, I enjoyed it." She walked over to him and put her hand on his shoulder, causing him to stop his nervous pacing.

"God! I want you. I lose control around you," he said, running his hands up her arms and then dipping his head for a small kiss.

"Walk me home?" Megan smiled up at him.

"How about a ride?" Todd said with a grin.

"I thought you'd never ask." Chester pushed against Todd's shoulders again and they both laughed.

Chapter Seven

It had been weeks since Megan had visited Matt's gravesite. The black marble marker had been set in place, and the white lilies she'd brought sat in the dark marble vase.

"Matt, I didn't mean to hide my life from you. I just couldn't bear it if…if you were disappointed in me." She closed her eyes on a tear. "I was so ashamed of myself, Matt, that I couldn't function. I…I didn't function as a human being. I let someone else control every part of me. At times, I felt like I would fade away and blend into the walls."

She opened her eyes and looked around the cemetery.

"Never again. I promise you and myself, never again." Letting out a breath, she felt a warm breeze lift over her. "I like it here and I like the people, especially the Jordan family. Oh, Matt, I can see now how easy it was for you to become so attached to them."

Megan smiled. "Lacey is wonderful. She's full of spunk and so very strong for such a small thing. Iian is kind and reminds me a lot of you. He makes me laugh and helps me forget all the bad things in my past. Then there's Todd." She paused and remembered last night and heat spread through her body.

"Matt, I don't know whether I can ever trust another man completely. I hope one day I won't be so damaged. That I'm able to feel alive again, because Todd makes me feel alive, and he deserves something more. I don't know if I'm capable of giving it to him. I miss you." Wiping the tear from her cheek, she turned and walked back to her car.

Late one evening, Megan arrived home from working at the cabins to see Lacey's car parked in the driveway. She walked into the house to find Lacey standing in her kitchen, cooking something that smelled wonderful. She had on an old pair of jeans and an oversized sweater, and had thick, purple socks covering her feet. She was humming to herself. Without turning around, Lacey said, "Hi. I thought you might like some dinner, and since it's my night off, I figured we could have a girls' night."

"That sounds great!" Megan plopped down in the kitchen chair. "I never knew there was so much to fixing a place up. I don't want to look at another paint brush for a year." Lacey smiled over at her. "Speaking of paint, do you know Allison Adams? She runs that little antique store across from the hardware store?"

"I use to babysit her and her sister, Abby. Abby passed away a few years back. She had cancer," Lacey said, sounding sad.

"Oh no, I didn't know that. That's too bad." Megan felt even closer to Allison, knowing they'd both lost their only sibling. "She does some of the most beautiful paintings and sketches. I've bought a few. I have some here in the house, and I'm going to hang some in the cabins."

"I didn't know she painted at all."

Megan walked over to the refrigerator and pulled out a bottle of wine she'd been saving. "She seemed so lonely when I was over there last week. We ended up talking for about two hours, and then she came over the other night and helped me hang up the paintings." Megan poured two glasses and handed one to Lacey. "I'm thinking of helping her market some of her art, you know, help her get it into galleries. I did some work a while back for this small art gallery in Portland. The owner was really nice to me, so I called him the other day and he said he's interested in seeing some of her stuff."

Lacey smiled over at Megan. "You really are a lot like your brother."

"You know, Iian was here when Allison arrived," she said with a hint of humor.

"How did that go?" Lacey said, turning around and giving Megan her full attention. "Was he nervous?" Lacey asked.

"Boy, was he! What is that all about?" she asked before taking a sip of wine.

"Oh, Iian has had this thing for Allison since second grade. Iian gets all nervous around her. It's kind of cute."

"I would feel very flattered if a man got nervous around me." The two giggled together.

Girls' night was a success, full of laughter and talking. It felt good to have a girl around. Megan could tell that Lacey loved her brothers, but she mentioned that they could be bullheaded and overprotective.

"Gee, I think I need something to eat. This wine is going to my head. Here I've been rambling on and haven't let you get in a word."

Megan looked down and realized her second glass of wine was gone. She smiled. It would be good to get drunk—she hadn't done so in years—so she poured more. She did the same for Lacey

An hour later, the two were sitting on the living room floor, an empty bottle of wine and two empty plates sitting next to them.

She'd found Matt's old photo album, and they were laughing at the outfit she'd worn to a high school dance and at her date for the evening.

"Well, what do we have here?" A deep voice came from the doorway. Megan squealed and tipped over her empty glass.

Todd stood in the doorway, leaning against the frame. Both girls started laughing again, so much so, they fell over, holding their sides.

Todd had taken a walk to clear his mind and had somehow ended up on Megan's porch. He hadn't expected to find both Megan and his sister sprawled out on the living room floor, giggling like a couple of high school girls.

He'd stopped by her house almost every night since that night at the pond, looking for an excuse to come up to the house. Lacey's car in the driveway had given him one.

"I made dinner for Megan, and, well…" Lacey stifled a giggle. "We were looking at old pictures."

Todd grinned down at them. "So you decided to get smashed and look at old photos, eh?" He walked over and tried to get a look at the photo book, which Megan quickly snapped shut.

"Oh, no, you don't," she said with a shake of her head. She grabbed her head with her hands, as it to stop it from spinning. She looked up at him, but couldn't seem to focus on his face. She gave him a smile and held the book close to her chest.

Looking down at Megan sitting on the floor with a silly grin on her face, her hair messed up with her eyes out of focus, Todd lost his heart. She had looked beautiful before, but once she relaxed and stopped jumping at shadows, she was exquisite. He leaned over and helped Lacey to her feet before reaching for Megan.

He couldn't help himself from keeping his hands on Megan's hips a little longer than was necessary. He told himself it was just to make sure she was steady on her feet. The truth was he wanted to have his hands on her.

When he felt himself stirring, he quickly pulled away, almost causing her to topple over. Lacey had already sat on the couch and had laid her head on one of the pillows. Her eyes were droopy and her speech slurred. "Whew, I drank more than I should have. I'll just lie here for…" She closed her eyes and began to snore lightly.

Todd chuckled. His sister had never been able to hold her liquor. He looked over at Megan and assumed the same. Walking over, he pulled his sister's purple-socked feet up on the couch and tucked a quilt around her.

"I think zhez-a-zleep," Megan whispered, teetering on her feet. Todd wrapped his arms around her to steady her. "I never saw someone fall a-zleep so quickly." When he started to answer, she put her finger across his lips and shushed him.

He walked her out to the front porch. The weather had started to get warmer at nights; in a few weeks, they would see spring. Still, he removed his jacket and wrapped it around her. Her cast fit easily in the oversized sleeves. Todd helped her sit down on the wicker swing and pulled her close, putting his arm around her shoulders.

Megan sighed and leaned her head back on his shoulder. The night was clear and the stars were bright in the sky.

She sighed again. "I like your sister, I like your brother, I like you, I like your whole family." She turned her head to look into his eyes.

Heat spread through his body; he felt like he was on fire. Todd looked down at her, and he knew his eyes were burning.

The kiss started slowly. Her lips were warm and soft, and she tasted like wine and Lacey's famous red sauce. He rubbed his tongue lightly over her closed lips, parting them slightly so he could gently play with her tongue and taste the rich flavor. He cupped her face in his hands and took the kiss deeper. She tasted so good that he had to have more. He pulled her closer He moved his fingers to her hair and tilted her head back. His other hand inched over her body, torturing them both.

"I can't seem to get close enough," he said, reaching down and pulling the coat apart. He slid his fingers up to the soft skin under her shirt. He would think about the fact that they were sitting outside on her front porch like a couple of teenagers later. For now, all he wanted to think about was her. His fingers slid over her ribs to play with the soft lacy fabric she wore underneath her shirt. She was perfect. He molded his hand to her breast, weighing her, playing with her until her nipple was a tight peak under his fingers, then moved over and did the same to the other side.

He was drowning and thoroughly enjoying it. Her skin was cool against his heated hands. She leaned into his palm as he played lightly with her. She pressed her body boldly against him, causing a moan to escape his mouth. She was wreaking havoc on his system.

She played over the muscles in his shoulders with her fingertips, and then moved up to his hair, keeping his head to her. She nipped at his lips and when she sucked on his bottom lip, pulling it into her mouth, he wanted to take her then and there. He knew he had to stop. His sister was on the couch in the next room. It was the hardest thing he'd ever had to do, but he moved back slowly, giving Megan time to adjust. He put the coat back over her shoulder, closing the warm air in and leaving him out. He looked down at her upturned face. Her eyes were still closed and her lips were swollen from his, but a smile played at the corners. He wanted to carry her upstairs and peel the clothes from her slowly, but now was not the time.

"Mm, you taste good," Megan hummed. "More?" she said, leaning towards him.

"No." He knew his words were like ice water since she blinked and sat up, pulling herself from him. "Don't," he said when he felt her pull away. "It's not that. It's just…my God, I want you so much." He rubbed his hands up and down her arms to please himself. "Lacey is asleep on the couch, right inside that door. We have plenty of time to pursue this."

She nodded, then leaned back into him and relaxed. Her body felt soft and warm next to his. "I want you too." She sighed and fell asleep against his shoulder.

Todd sat there, letting his mind wander, with her body heating his in so many ways, wanting her even more. When Megan began to stir, he quietly carried her up the stairs and laid her on the bed, then pulled the comforter over her. He gently pushed some of her hair from her forehead, and when she sighed, he knew he'd lost his heart. All he wanted now was to see a smile on her lips every day and make sure her eyes never went wide with fright again.

When Sara had died, he'd gone through depression, then anger, then resentment. He was at a point in his life where he wanted to live it to the fullest. His life needed purpose: a wife, children. He'd really been looking forward to having a little one when Sara and the child had died. In truth, he had mourned more for the child than for Sara.

But now, as he drove himself home in Lacey's car, an image of Megan in his arms kept running through his brain. It had been a long time since he'd felt alive around someone. It was about time.

Chapter Eight

Megan woke to a thousand pins sticking in her head. She vaguely heard someone banging around in the kitchen below. For a minute, she thought she was back in Boston and that Derek would walk in any moment, demanding she get her lazy ass out of bed.

Then she heard the birds outside her window, and she smelled Todd and relaxed. Sitting up in bed, she realized she was still fully clothed and clenching Todd's coat.

Taking a big breath, she breathed him in and felt a stir in her stomach. How could a man do this to her just with his scent? She hadn't come here wanting this, but she couldn't deny what he did to her, either. She felt something for him, that was for sure. Every time he was around, her palms got damp and her heart raced.

She got up from the bed with a grunt, her head spun, and then the world righted itself. After taking two aspirin and a quick bath and brushing her teeth, she almost felt human again. She pulled on a pair of sweats and another of Matt's shirts, then combed through her wet hair and headed downstairs.

She had expected to see Lacey in the kitchen, banging the pots and pans. Instead, Lacey sat at the table with her face down, moaning. She had a cup of coffee in one hand and a glass with a reddish-orange liquid in the other.

Megan looked over at the stove and stopped. Todd stood there in her lacy white apron with a spatula in one hand and a cup of coffee in the other. "I thought you girls might need a little pick-me-up today. How do blueberry pancakes sound?" When Lacey moaned loudly, he chuckled.

"Actually, that sounds great," Megan said, walking over to the table as Todd set the mug down in front of her. The coffee was hot and strong, just the way she liked it. "You know, I think I'm getting spoiled. Since I've been here, I've only had to fend for myself for about three meals." She gave Todd a smile and sipped her coffee.

The sun was shining, the birds were singing, and she was eating homemade blueberry pancakes for the first time since she was nine. Not to mention actually feeling like she was part of a family, something, no matter how hard Matt had ever tried, she hadn't felt in a long time.

They ate pancakes and talked about the work that had been done and still needed to be done on the cabins.

The walls were completed on the farthest one. She called it the honeymoon cabin. It was farthest from the main house in a more private, secluded area surrounded by trees. She'd picked out romantic furnishings and had found some lace window coverings that let in plenty of light.

She set aside some of Allison's watercolors to hang up throughout the other cabins. She had statues and some bowls picked out from Allison's store, knowing they would look perfect.

One of the other cabins was going to be decorated to match one of Allison's paintings, the dancing fairies. She'd picked a forest green for the window coverings and had painted the walls a dark cream. In all the other rooms, she'd used darker neutral colors. She wanted the paintings to make a statement, not the walls. She needed to finish painting in that cabin today. The plumber should be there already, working on the sinks and the toilet.

The larger items, including her new hot tub, would be delivered the day after tomorrow. The furniture in storage would be delivered the day after that.

She was excited to see what furniture Matt had picked out and whether it would go along with the themes she'd chosen. If it didn't, she could always swap out what she had at the main house to accommodate.

She had decided on advertising on the menus at the restaurant, and Iian had told her they would go to print and should be ready in less than a week.

She also had an ad ready for the Portland newspaper and was working with an old colleague to get an ad online. There was a possibility of working with a travel agency she'd done some marketing for a couple of years back, as well.

Matt had had a separate phone line installed in his office that she could use to answer for the rentals. She would still need a computer program to help her track the rentals, and there was the matter of taxes.

"How are taxes paid for small businesses in Oregon?" she asked Todd while they were cleaning away the table.

"There are some forms that need to be filled out. I think Matt had already completed them. We can have a look," he said. "They would be in his office somewhere. Think you can handle the rest of the dishes, Lacey?"

"Sure, go have fun. I have to go home and get ready for work tonight, anyway." She gave Megan a hug. "I would love to help you finish shopping, you know, to fill in the holes here and there. Let me know when you're ready to spend a day hitting the stores."

"That sounds great. I'll let you know when everything's ready."

Todd and Megan spent the next hour with their heads bent over the computer and the paperwork Matt had filled out. He'd taken care of the taxes and the business registration. He had also obtained a website and had hired a local company to design it. When Todd called the company, they informed him they were only waiting for pictures of the cabins and the surrounding area before the site could go live. Megan needed to buy a digital camera.

"We could drive into Portland to get you one."

"Well, I do need to finish painting both bedrooms in the second cabin." Megan chewed her bottom lip. "But I guess if I could stop by my friend's art gallery while I'm there…"

"Art gallery?" Todd asked.

"Oh, I know the owner of this art gallery in Portland. I wanted to see if putting some of Allison Adams's artwork in his gallery was a possibility."

"Well, if you know where the gallery is, we can get on Google and find out where the nearest camera store is."

Megan pulled up the address in her day planner and gave it to him. “I’ll go change,” she said, looking down at the sweats she’d pulled on this morning.

When she headed upstairs, she could hear Todd clicking away at the keyboard. It was nice to have someone to work with. It didn’t hurt that he was a hunk and made her heart flutter. It would be wonderful spending the day in Portland. She missed the bustle of a city.

Half an hour later, armed with four of Allison’s smaller paintings and directions to both the art gallery and a couple of camera stores nearby, Todd and Megan headed out. They decided to take the Jeep so the paintings would easily fit in the back.

With Todd behind the wheel, the drive was very relaxing. Megan felt like she was seeing the countryside for the first time. The drive from the airport had been a slow one filled with maps and rain. Today the sun was out and there was hardly a cloud in the sky. She could see for miles.

“You don’t find it a little crowded? Living with your sister and brother?” Megan asked, looking over at him.

“No, it’s nice being close.” He chuckled a little and then sobered. “It really helped after the accident, adjusting and all. We hired a tutor to teach us sign language together. I've noticed you're picking it up fast. If you want to learn more, I can help."

"Oh, that would be great. I feel so left out sometimes. You guys seem so close. Has it always been that way?" she asked.

"No. Lacey and I've always been close, but Iian and I had a falling out right before Sara died. He was young, I was arrogant…You know." He shrugged his shoulders.

"Matt and I had a fight the last time he came out," Megan said, looking down at her arm. She'd grown accustomed to fidgeting with the ends of the cast. "I feel really bad. We did set things right over the phone, but the last time I saw him…" Tears came back to her eyes.

"Don't do that. You know your brother loved you; he would have forgiven you for anything. I'm sure he'd long forgotten about whatever it was. You should do the same. Now, tell me about these paintings. How did you get little Allison Adams to sell you these?" He changed the subject so quickly Megan had to stifle a laugh. Obviously, Todd didn't handle weeping women well.

"Well, I went into her store a couple of weeks back to get some items for the cabins and noticed them in the back room. I guess I just kind of barged in and started buying the ones I liked. I'd done some marketing work for Mr. Derby—that's the owner of the Blue Spot Gallery—and he was very kind over the phone. I haven't met him personally, but last week when I called, he was excited I was nearby. He said he was going to be in Portland for the next few months and to bring some of Allison's work up if I got the chance."

"That's very nice of you to help her out. I'm pretty impressed by what you have planned for the bed-and-breakfast. You have some talent pulling a business together. We could use your help with the restaurant. That is, if you want to. Your brother helped me out a lot with my company, but since then, it's moved to a whole different level."

"I never thought he would settle down in a place like Pride."

"Why not?" Todd asked, looking over at her.

"Matt was—well, to put it bluntly—a wanderer. He never stayed in one place long enough to put down roots. Ever since I can remember, he was uprooting me from schools. We mostly stayed in the Boston area during the school year. I remember one year he got it in his head that he would homeschool me so we could travel year round." Megan giggled. "Then he took one look at my algebra book, and the next day, I was enrolled in school and he had signed a lease on an apartment down the street."

Todd smiled back at her. "Well, he settled pretty well here. He did travel a lot the first year, but the main house wasn't quite done being remodeled. He was really concerned about you near the end and wanted to start the bed-and-breakfast with you. His goal was to get you focused on it so he could persuade you to move here."

"I would have eventually, but I really needed to find myself first." Megan turned her head and looked out the window.

"Is that what you're doing now, finding yourself?"

She could see the question he wanted to ask her written on his face. "No," she said softly. "I'm reinventing myself."

"Had things become so bad that you needed to reinvent yourself?" He looked over at her.

"I let things in my life control me. I want to know that I can do this, that I'm still alive. I know your family has been tiptoeing around the fact I've been hurt," she said. "I know I should talk about it, and I really want to, but there's so much I am ashamed of."

"You've nothing to be ashamed of," Todd said quickly. Megan sat up, trying to mask the hurt in her face. "Damn it," Todd said quietly, steering the car towards the shoulder. He was staring down at his knuckles, which were turning white on the steering wheel. "I know what you've been through. I can see it all over your face. I know who did it to you too. That's clear as well. I can't begin to comprehend why he did it or fathom what you went through, but I am here to listen." He looked over at her. "I can't promise not to show emotion because, to be honest, it just pisses me off, seeing the aftermath. But I'm not mad at you, never at you." He turned his body towards her, but she had her eyes fixed on her fingers. She was still messing with the end of the cast. He reached over and put her hand in his. "Let's get some lunch. I want to hear your story, if you'll tell it." When Megan nodded, he pulled the jeep back on the road.

They found a small sandwich shop ten minutes later. It was warm, so they sat outside at a covered table and ate in silence. When she'd eaten her turkey sandwich, she relaxed and began to talk.

Chapter Nine

"I met Derek in college when I was a freshman. He was a senior about to graduate with a pre-law degree. I thought I'd found the man I wanted to grow old with, and we married less than a year later. The wedding was small and wonderful, and I thought it would be the start of a really great life. That night, our wedding night, I learned it wasn't to be a dream but a nightmare. Derek was very upset about some of the college friends I'd invited to the wedding. That was the first time he hit me. Things progressed from there. He wasn't only controlling, he was extremely jealous. I learned his moods, learned when to keep my mouth shut, learned to apologize for everything, whether I'd done anything wrong or not. One night, my boss at Martin and Marcus, the marketing firm I worked for, needed me to stay late on a campaign that was due to go to print the next day. Actually, it was Ric Derby's gallery campaign I was working on. You have to understand, my boss Jose was a sixty-five-year-old grandfather of six. He was like a father figure to me.

"When I got home late that night, Derek accused me of having an affair. Things escalated from there, and I woke up in the hospital with him standing over me, telling an officer how I'd been mugged in the parking lot of our complex. I had sixteen stitches to my head, three broken ribs, and two broken fingers." Megan looked down now at her hand. Her fingers were healed, but they still ached when it got cold.

"When I was released, he bought me diamond earrings and apologized. He told me he was under a lot of stress from work, and he wouldn't be able to stand it if I left him. I regularly got slapped or pushed. He started throwing things at me too; he had really good aim. He started with small items—shoes, books—and then he started in on the lamps and small furniture. After the third time I ended up in the hospital, someone called the police since his excuses weren't believable anymore. They couldn't arrest him unless I pressed charges. I took their advice and moved into a shelter. I was there for two weeks when Derek found me and dragged me back; then he kept me locked up in a room, a prisoner." She looked up at Todd.

He sat patiently, listening. His knuckles where white, but his face showed little emotion. She could tell he was struggling to keep it in check. "He'd taken me to a remote run-down motel that rented by the week. I was locked in the same room for three days, no phone, no going out, little to no food since he was at work all day, and all I could eat was what he gave me. He'd even paid the staff not to bother us or stop by to clean our room. He'd installed a lock on the outside of the bathroom door and locked me in it every day. Even when he was there, I spent most of my time locked in the tiny space. It was a six-by-seven room, no windows, no fresh air. I was going crazy. I thought there was no way out."

"And then, one day, the bathroom door just pushed open. Maybe he'd forgotten to lock it, I don't know, but I ran. I didn't even grab clothes. I ran to the corner and then to the next and then the next. I ended up about six miles away at a Quick-N-Stop. I called my boss and asked if he could come take me to the police station. Mr. Martin helped me file for divorce and get a restraining order against Derek. I formally pressed charges, and they arrested him and sentenced him to two years in prison, but he only served six months. Part of the plea bargain was based on him signing the divorce papers. After I recovered, I started back at work. Mr. Martin hired me back, no questions asked. I sold the townhouse, signed a lease on a new apartment on the other side of town, bought new furniture…I thought I'd started my new life."

Todd reached over and held her left hand; she'd been peeling the cast away again. She'd been talking without really seeing him, trying not to show emotion.

"The restraining order was still in effect. He couldn't get within two hundred feet of me, and he stayed away for a while, until a week before Matt died. I'd been putting in some extra hours, trying to save up for a trip back here to visit. When I got home that night, I remember turning around to lock the door, and he was just…there. I guess my neighbor called the police when she saw him push his way in. It took them ten minutes to get there. If they hadn't arrived so quickly, I would be dead. Derek hadn't changed. He told me I had ruined his life. He said he knew I'd been sleeping around, and I deserved everything I'd gotten and more. That if he couldn't have me, then no one would, and I needed to pay for all the damage I'd done to his career."

She held up her right arm. "This happened when I tried to push him out the door. He just—snapped it. He pushed me in and locked the door so we wouldn't be 'interrupted.' Within five minutes, he had broken almost all the items in my living room, claiming that someone must have bought everything for me since I was too stupid to survive without him. Then he started in on me. I had edged my way towards the kitchen phone. He looked up from smashing my new television and noticed me. The bruises on my back are from one of my kitchen chairs."

Todd's hand tightened around hers, not painfully, but enough that it snapped Megan from her trance.

"Todd, I'm sorry." She blinked again.

"Don't!" he said quickly. "You've nothing to be sorry for. At least tell me the bastard is locked up for good."

"Yes, for now. The trial is set for sometime late next month. My lawyer says I won't have to testify. I try to imagine it was someone else's life, like watching a movie, that it really didn't happen to me. Then I move the wrong way and the pain comes back. I went to a counselor right after he was sentenced the first time. She helped me deal with a lot of the hurt. I felt as if it was all my fault. I would look around and see happy couples holding hands, kissing, and here I was, abused and torn down. What did I do wrong? Why did these other women get their happy ever after, and I got—well, not. It must be me, right? Derek would constantly tell me what was wrong with me. I didn't think before I said something; I didn't say it nicely enough or in the right tone. I had no sense of style, I didn't walk feminine enough, or put on enough makeup, and then I put too much on and looked like a tramp and so on."

"Stop! There isn't a thing wrong with you."

"I know. At least I'm beginning to understand it wasn't me, it was him. At one point, my self-esteem was so low, I thought of hurting myself. Anything to make the pain stop. Every time I would think that way, I'd remember my father. Then I would think of Matt's face and…well…I couldn't leave him alone."

"Why didn't you ever tell Matt what was happening? You know he would have helped."

"At first it was shame. Then it grew to something else. I don't know. I guess I wanted him to be proud of me, and well, how can you expect someone to be proud of you when you're not proud of yourself?"

"I think he would be very proud of you now. You're a survivor. Just look at what you've done, what you survived. Not only are you starting your own business, you're helping market a local artist. You've befriended the entire town. You're not only the smartest woman I know, you happen to be the prettiest." Todd stood and pulled her up to him, holding her tight against his chest. "It kills me to hear what you've gone through. I wish I could take it all away. Don't ever doubt yourself, Megan. You're incredible."

Megan held on and smiled. It was nice to have someone believe in her. Life looked better in Todd's arms. His muscles bunched in his back when she grabbed on to him. He felt powerful and she explored his back with her hands.

"I think you're pretty incredible too," she said against his chest.

"Shall we get going? These paintings won't sell themselves."

Megan pulled away, but before she could move, he captured her lips in a soft kiss. The kiss said so much that Megan was shaking when he finally moved away.

As they finished the short drive into the city, she couldn't help but wonder about him. He'd made it very clear that he wanted her physically, but she had the feeling he kept a distance between them. Almost like he was unsure he could trust himself with her.

She'd only been in two serious relationships in her life; one had ended badly and the other had ended worse. She knew relationships could be good and there could be mutual gain. At least that was what most magazines said about them. She'd never experienced this firsthand and found it odd that a man could think of a woman as an equal in relationships. Derek had treated her more like his property. Her father had never really treated her mother like she was worth anything from what she could remember.

They finally pulled up in front of the Blue Spot Gallery. It sat on Main Street in an older part of Portland, a three-story brick building that was over a hundred years old. The Blue Spot Gallery and the surrounding buildings had been remodeled, so they looked classic. Long windows covered the front of the building. Several paintings hung in the left window, and a black-and-white picture of a child holding a tulip covered the other. The gallery was very impressive.

As they walked in, a woman in her fifties came over to them. She had her hair pulled up in a tight bun and wore a simple brown business suit. "Welcome to the Blue Spot Gallery. Is there anything in particular I can help you with today?"

"Yes, this is Megan Kimble, and I'm Todd Jordan. We're here to see Mr. Derby."

"Yes, Miss Kimble, Mr. Derby has been expecting you. Please feel free to look around while I inform him you're here." She walked over to a small desk and picked up a phone.

The art covering the walls ranged from exquisite to very odd. While Todd and Megan moved around, talking about some of the paintings, Ric watched the good-looking couple from above.

So, this was Megan Kimble? She was younger and prettier than he'd imagined. Because of this woman's genius marketing plans, the Blue Spot Galleries had been able to expand all the way to New York. She'd worked quickly and efficiently, and he had a great deal of respect for her. He'd imagined her as a whirlwind of energy.

But now, standing in his gallery, she looked small and somewhat lost. The broken arm left her looking vulnerable. His assistant had told him that the man she was with was Mr. Todd Jordan. Ric had heard of him, the owner of Jordan Shipping. Ric used his company to ship paintings and some of the larger art pieces around the world.

But what was Megan Kimble doing with Todd Jordan? Just then, he saw Todd lean over and whisper something in Megan's ear that made her giggle.

Instantly, he felt respect for the man. Megan Kimble had been through hell. Ric didn't know the whole story, but Mr. Martin had explained why she hadn't shown up for the conference in New York several years back. Ric had also heard the despair in her voice every time they talked over the phone.

He walked forward to greet the woman to whom he owed everything. "Megan?"

Megan turned to see a bronzed man in his late twenties. He was about six feet tall with neatly cut blond hair. He wore a black suit and a bright blue tie. She'd imagined he would look just like this.

His smooth voice had soothed her when there had been little hope in her life. In truth, she'd become very close to this man during the seven months they'd worked together over the phone. She'd had the opportunity to meet him in person once in New York, but she hadn't ended up going due to a black eye and swollen lip.

"Ric, it's so good to finally meet you," Megan said, shaking his left hand. "This is Todd Jordan, my good friend and neighbor."

"Mr. Jordan." They shook hands as well, but Megan could see something spark in Ric's eyes. "It's a great pleasure to meet you. I've used your company for the last couple years with no complaints."

"Thank you. It's a lovely place you have here. Megan tells me you have several other galleries."

"Yes, one in Seattle, two in California, one in New York. Won't you come up to my office? We can have some refreshments."

"Oh, that would be fine. I've brought those paintings we talked about. They're out in the car," Megan said.

"I'll go grab them," Todd said, starting out.

"So, Megan, tell me more about this bed-and-breakfast of yours." Ric gently cupped her left elbow and started walking towards the stairs. By the time they reached the landing, Todd was starting up the stairs with several paintings tucked under his arm.

Once in the office, Ric motioned for her to sit. Taking the paintings from Todd, he set them down on an easel beside a desk.

"So, tell me about this artist," he said as he stood in front of one of Allison's paintings. It was a small portrait of a pixie that sat hunched over on a rock in a pond. Her wings were tucked down, and she stared at her reflection in the water. Megan thought she looked remarkably like Lacey.

"Well, she's from Pride, and she works with oil, watercolors, charcoal, and pencil. I've only known her since I've been there, but I've purchased several of her pieces for my bed-and-breakfast."

Ric moved from painting to painting. When Mrs. Barns came in with the tea, he continued to look at the painting. He hadn't spoken, and the room sat silent for a few minutes. Then he abruptly sat behind his desk, his eyes still on the pixie.

"She has talent, that is clear. I'd like to meet her and see more of her work. I'm very interested in showing it. Does she have an agent?"

Megan was taken aback. "Really? I mean, wow, yes, no, I mean she doesn't have an agent. Maybe you can suggest someone for her?"

Ric smiled. "Yes, as a matter of fact, I've several. First off, though, I would like to display these paintings in the gallery, if they are still available."

"Oh, well, you'll have to take that up with Allison. I'm just borrowing these." Megan looked over at Todd. "You see, she doesn't think anyone would be interested in her work."

"I can assure you they will be. Actually, I'd like this one"—he said, pointing to the pixie by the pond—"for myself. I think I know a buyer for two of the other oils, and as for the watercolor, I'm sure it would sell within the first week. Do you happen to have Allison's number? We'll give her a quick call."

Allison sounded shocked and excited over the phone. She agreed to meet with Ric next week at her store so he could take a look at the rest of her work. He gave her several names and numbers for some local agents and assured her he would have them contact her before next week.

By the time Todd and Megan walked out of the gallery, Megan's head was spinning. Not only would Ric be displaying Allison's artwork, but he'd arranged for a photographer by the name of Brad Stone to stop by later in the week to take professional pictures of the cabins for her. Ric had also suggested that she mail some of the completed brochures to him so he could post them in each of his galleries.

Because they no longer needed to hit the camera stores, they checked out some of the local sights. They hit a lot of shops and when they came to a little bookstore, Megan pulled Todd inside.

"I've been meaning to find some books." Todd cringed a little but then relaxed when she took him to the home-improvement section. She chuckled to herself. He'd probably thought she was going to make him look at romance novels.

By the time they walked out, she had a stack of how-to books for gardening, painting, and deck and hot tub care. She had also picked up a picture book of Portland that she would put in one of the cabins and a beginner's guide to sign language.

Megan had never felt so free. Never had she spent a more relaxed day. Todd was great company, and he didn't complain about any of the little stores she dragged him into. By the time they headed back to the Jeep, they both had their hands full of bags.

Chapter Ten

The drive back was peaceful. They chatted about everything and nothing. The sun was setting when they finally drove up to the house and Todd parked the Jeep in the garage.

"When do you get your cast removed?" he asked, helping her into the house with her packages.

"It should come off in a few days. I'll need to find a local doctor to remove it. Do you know of anyone?"

"Yes, Dr. Stevens has been the town's doctor since before I was born. He patched up Iian and me more times than I can count. His office is across from the library. If you set an appointment, I can drive you down there."

They walked into the house and were halfway across the living room before they realized Iian sat at the dining room table with a pile of papers spread out.

"Oh no, Iian! I'm sorry. I forgot about our meeting." She looked over at Todd. "We were going to go over the new menus for the bed-and-breakfast." Iian took one look at Todd and shoved up from the table, smiling.

"It's all right. I understand," he said, walking to the door. Halfway there, Megan caught up with him and pulled on his arm until he turned around.

"I'm truly sorry. We went into Portland to purchase a camera and, well, we dropped by a friend's art gallery, and I guess I got so caught up in the day, I forgot about our meeting."

"Megan," he said, taking her hand in his, "you don't have to explain. Why don't we meet tomorrow afternoon? I've left a list of possible menu items on the table. Look them over and we can discuss them tomorrow." He looked over her head at his brother and nodded with a funny smile. "Good night." Then he was gone.

"I didn't mean to hurt his feelings. I just forgot," Megan said, turning back towards Todd, who still had a handful of bags and boxes.

"He really has it bad for you," Todd murmured with a slight smile. Megan bit her bottom lip with worry, and he dropped the packages on the table and walked over to her. "He'll get over it. Iian falls for a new woman every month. Last month it was Mary, the vet who takes care of Chester. Don't worry, he'll be fine." Todd didn't want the night to end just yet. "How about I make you some dinner? I make a mean peanut butter and jelly sandwich."

"Yum, sounds good. You make the sandwiches, and I'll make some tomato soup." She said.

"Well," he said, putting his hands on her hips and pulling her closer. "I don't know. How good is your soup?" He leaned in a little more.

"The best that Campbell's has to offer." She stretched up on her toes and gave him a light kiss. When she started to pull back, he held her closer, pulling her mouth back to his.

"I love the taste of you." The kiss was light and playful to begin with but then it grew more desperate. He grew more desperate. His tongue reached deep inside, dueling with Megan's. Her arm was around his shoulders. She reached up and held his head to hers. She curled her fingers in his hair to keep his mouth to hers.

"More," she said in a husky voice.

He could no longer control himself, and his shoulders shook as he ran his hands up and down her spine. She was so soft in his arms. The cast was in the way, so he moved it to her side, giving himself the pleasure of running his mouth over her neck, gently taking her earlobe in his mouth and nibbling. She let out a long sigh. He had to have more. He backed her up until her knees hit the couch and then moved down with her, laying her gently on the cushions.

He reached up to the soft skin under her blouse. His fingers searched each rib, tickling her skin but making her moan with pleasure.

Finally, he reached the lacy material of her bra and searched underneath for the tight bud that rose and hardened at his light touch. She bucked underneath him and sent her own hand on a search below his shirt.

He opened her shirt and brought his mouth to her breast, his tongue swirling around her tight bud. He took it in his mouth and began to suck lightly, using his teeth and tongue to please her.

Her nails dug into his shoulders, then, reaching down, she untucked his shirt from his jeans. It must have been hard to do with only one hand. When he noticed her struggling, he sat up quickly to remove his shirt for her, pulling hers away as well. He had some difficulty moving it over the cast, and she had to sit up and help him. She gave a little nervous laugh when he looked at her.

"I want you so much, Megan. Don't make me go home tonight."

"No, stay," she said and moved him back down. Their kisses were hungrier than before.

He moved her bra straps down her shoulders, putting his hands over the rosy buds and gently pulling. She squirmed under him, causing his arousal to push up against her hip.

He unbuttoned her slacks, running his fingers lightly down her hip until he reached the lace there. Moving it aside, he reached into the soft curls. She was hot and wet when he parted her soft skin and began to play. She bucked again as her hips moved into his hand.

Running her hand down his chest and over his tight stomach muscles, she reached for his jeans. Then she ran her fingertips lightly over him, rubbing the coarse denim stretched over him, until he thought his eyes would cross. When she started to reach for the button, he moved her hand away.

"Megan, my God! I need a minute, please, let me…" he said against her neck.

"No, now, please, Todd. I won't break. Help me."

He was lost. He pulled her up and yanked her slacks and panties off in one quick movement. Then he was out of his own jeans and lying her back on the couch before she could appreciate the full view.

"I won't hurt you," he said, looking into her eyes.

He gently pushed her legs up and apart. She looked back into his eyes and nodded. "No, never!"

she said, running her hand down his side until she reached his butt. She pulled him to her as he plunged into her heat.

There were two equal moans of delight. He held still; the only sound now was their joined breath. They stopped moving as they looking into each other's eyes for what seemed like an eternity, his weight pinning her to the cushions and his body heating hers.

Then, when he thought he couldn't hold back anymore, she moved under him, her hips rotating and lifting, and the last thread of his control snapped. It had never been like this. She was so hot. As he reached down between their bodies, she screamed out his name and lost herself, and he could feel her body slowly melting against his.

He pulled her up and slid his mouth against her heated skin, tasting her as he buried his mouth against her core. She moaned and grabbed his head. His tongue darted inside her to lick the sweet arousal.

"Todd, I don't, I can't…" She ended on a moan.

When her hips started pumping against his mouth, he pulled himself back up and plunged into her again, running his tongue over her earlobe, lightly sucking on it.

His muscles bunched under her light touch. He left a blazing trail over her body with his mouth.

She was so hot, it felt like his lungs were on fire from looking at her. Her kisses drugged him to the point of oblivion. The speed and heat from her body built, and he knew she found as much pleasure as he did.

She felt something inside of her that she'd never felt before. It started deep in her chest and rose to her throat. Closing her eyes, she threw back her head and fell just as he did.

She must have slept, warm and sated, with his weight pinning her to the sofa. When he moved, she tried to pull him back down.

"I'll start a fire," he said, pulling a quilt from the back of the couch and covering her.

She rolled to her side and watched him bend over to light the wood. It was dark in the room, but she could make out his form. He seemed comfortable walking around naked. He had a great butt, she thought, and giggled into the quilt.

"And what would be so funny?" he asked, looking over his shoulder. The fire had started and was quickly building.

"You, me, this whole night. I've never done anything like this before." When Todd gave her a questioning look, she continued. "Well, I've done this before, just nothing like—you know." She felt shy all of a sudden, like a schoolgirl. How stupid could she get? She started to pull the blanket up over her face.

He reached her in two steps. "No, don't. I like to see you blush," he said, smiling down at her. He sat next to her and pulled her body to his so they could spoon on the sofa. She quickly tucked the quilt around them as they lay down facing the fire, her head tucked on his shoulder.

"It's just, well, I've only been with one other man and…" She trailed off, gazing into the fire. "It was never like that."

He kissed her hair. "When I'm around you, it's as if I've lost all control of my senses." He pulled her closer, as they watched the fire dance in the fireplace.

"What are you doing tomorrow?" he asked, running her hair slowly between his fingers. He loved the feeling.

She wanted to see him, but she needed some time to think about her future; she hadn't planned for something like this to happen to her. She wanted to focus on starting a new life. She knew dating was a possibility, but what she was starting to feel for Todd scared her.

"I really have to finish painting the cabins, finish getting them ready, and I have the meeting with your brother," she mumbled against his arm.

"Good, then we'll make a day of it." He continued to play with her hair. "You shouldn't be doing all this by yourself with a broken arm. Besides, I have nothing better to do tomorrow. I would like to help you." He kissed the side of her neck, trailing his mouth up to her ear, his hands playing over her ribs beneath the blanket.

How could she refuse him? "Your family has done so much for me. I feel like I owe you guys so much." He ran his hands over her, lighting little fires that caused her skin to tingle. Lightly, he kept tracing her ribs, all the while raining kisses along her neck. He was very soft and gentle with her. It almost brought tears to her eyes. She shut them on a moan. She started to turn around to face him, but he held her in place as his hand moved down to find her core, pressing his fingers to her. She started to grind her hips against him.

He was perfect. He was hard as he pressed against her back. She couldn't seem to get enough, and when he moved his hand down to her hip, pulling her against him, she moaned. She felt hot and wet as he lightly stroked her. He ran his fingers gently down, lingering just where she wanted, teasing her until she could feel the need change within her.. Pulling her leg up, he slowly sheathed himself inside her heat.

She reached up behind her and pulled his head down into her neck. His kisses soothed the skin below her ear. She found it difficult to breathe. His fingers roamed over her, possessing every part of her, cupping her breasts and tugging on the tight peaks until she moaned. Then his hands slowly traveled the length of her body, reaching her soft folds. She lost control and cried out his name.

Chapter Eleven

Megan woke to warm breath on her face. She'd somehow ended up sleeping on her stomach on top of Todd's chest. Now, as the morning light streamed in the windows, his breath raised goose bumps on her neck. She leaned up on her good arm and looked at him. It had been dark last night but today, in the light, she could enjoy the full view.

He continued to breathe heavily as she straddled him and took in her fill. He was a very good-looking man. His shoulders were wider than hers and packed with lean muscles. His stomach was tight with a perfect six-pack. A light cover of dark hair trailed downward.

A lock of his messed-up hair fell on his forehead. She itched to gently move it aside. When he continued to breathe deeply, she pushed his hair aside, running her fingers down his jaw. His face was smooth with the exception of a light growth from a night without shaving.

Smiling, she traced his neckline, letting her fingers walk down towards his chest, playing with the muscles and the light cover of hair. She let her fingers travel farther down his stomach, playing with each rib. When she moved her fingers over a particular rib, she thought she heard him suck in his breath, but when she looked at his face, his eyes were still closed and his breathing level.

She continued her downward path. She knew most men woke hard and ready, but she'd never experienced it before, let alone with someone she wanted to be with. Smiling to herself, she remembered how he felt inside her. She moved up on her knees until she could press her heat to his, then slowly, very slowly, she slid down until she was fully impaled. She threw her head back and ran her hand up her body, feeling totally wanton. And then she started to move.

Of course, Todd had awakened when she sat up. He knew she was looking at him and decided to let her take control.

It was complete torture when her fingers played lightly over his body. He'd been dreaming of making love to her again, so he woke hard, but when she started running her hands over him, he grew even more so.

When she pushed herself up on her knees, he thought she meant to leave. He was about to grab her hips to pull her back to him when she reached down and adjusted him to fit inside her as she slid slowly downwards. She started to rock her hips back and forth until he felt he could no longer control himself.

He reached up and cupped her hips, holding her down farther on him. She moved slowly and when he opened his eyes, she was running her hand down the length of her body, stopping just below her breasts. Reaching up, he put his hand over hers and ran them up so that she gripped herself.

Her eyes searched his own with uncertainty. He moved his hand to her right breast, mimicking her hold, and he pinched the bud ever so lightly. Her eyes widened and then, smiling, she mimicked his actions. He smiled back up at her and leaned up to replace his fingers with his mouth.

He'd meant to go slow, but his passion was building, and he found himself moving more rapidly. His hands went down to her hips and guided her at a faster pace.

He watched and knew that she could no longer hold back. She let go and cried out his name, then melted down to his chest.

Quickly switching positions so that she was beneath him, he pulled her legs up closer to his chest so she opened for him. Leaning over her, he took her mouth until she moaned and started moving again.

He was lost. He'd known she would be like this, soft and warm, but he never imagined she would be like a drug to his system, spreading throughout his entire being, intoxicating him until all he wanted to do was breathe her in.

She wrapped her legs around his hips and held on, and he took his fill of what she offered. Then his body went rigid and he whispered her name, spilling himself deep within.

"Good morning," he mumbled into her hair several minutes later.

Megan laughed and ran her hand up and pinched his butt. "You are a hard person to wake."

"Oh, is that what you were trying to do?" He laughed and looked down at her. Her hair was in tangles and her face was flushed. He'd never seen a more beautiful sight. "I suppose you want some breakfast, since we never got around to those sandwiches last night," he said as he pulled himself up.

Her stomach growled loudly in reply, causing him to laugh. He pulled on his jeans, leaving them unsnapped, and looked down at her. "Darling, if you don't go get cleaned up and dressed now, we might just spend the whole day on that couch."

She jumped up, tucking the blanket around her, and made a run for the stairs. She could hear Todd laughing as she made her way to her bedroom.

By the time she had bathed, combed her hair, and pulled on her painting jeans and T-shirt, she could smell bacon and coffee. Taking one last look at herself in the mirror, she paused; she'd never seen such a smile on her face.

Not that her whole life had been hard. But she'd been pushed into circumstances recently that had given her frown lines instead of laugh lines. Now, however, when she looked at herself in the mirror, she saw a young woman who had enjoyed her first real night of hot sex.

Jogging down the stairs, she heard Todd singing. She stepped into the kitchen and watched him. He was standing at the stove with her apron on, holding a spatula up to his mouth and singing *I've Got You Babe*. She let out a snort and laughed at him.

"Are you going to feed me or serenade me?" she asked, taking the cup of coffee he offered and downing two gulps. Todd scooped some eggs on a plate already full of bacon and toast and pushed her playfully into a chair.

"I've got to feed you if I'm to get any work out of you today." He sat down with a plate of eggs, bacon, and toast for himself.

Megan stared at her own plate. There was more food on it than she'd eat in an entire day.

Megan chuckled. "I'm wondering where the army is you were planning on feeding all this to."

"You haven't been eating well or sleeping," he said, scooping a big pile of eggs into his mouth. At her look, he said, "I worked up an appetite last night and this morning." He looked like a ten-year-old on Christmas morning.

"Goof," she said and scooped up her own eggs.

They did the dishes side by side, chatting about the work that needed to be done, and then packed a small lunch and headed out to the cabins. The walk was short and the clean air was great for clearing the mind.

Never had she spent a day with a man and so thoroughly enjoyed it. They laughed, joked, and flirted all day. They stopped for lunch and ended up sitting outside on the deck for longer than they expected. Todd was so easy to talk to that she didn't realize all the work was done and evening was quickly approaching.

Walking back towards the house, they held hands and chatted about small, meaningless things. Her porch light was on, and the place looked inviting, like home. Iian stood on the porch watching them and smiling.

Before they got too close, Todd stopped Megan, turning his back to his brother so he couldn't read what he was saying.

"I've got some things to take care of the next few days. Can you come for dinner tomorrow?"

Megan smiled. "Yes." She reached up on her toes and kissed him.

"Good night, then. I'll see you tomorrow." As Todd walked to his car, he signed to his smiling brother to mind his own business. He didn't like what Iian signed back, but he chuckled at the gesture and the fact that his brother had never kept his opinions to himself.

As he drove back to his house, he thought of the plans he wanted to make with Megan. He knew without a doubt he wanted her in his life. He just didn't know how she felt about it.

He also knew he needed to move slowly from here on out. She was everything he'd imagined and more. She was funny, smart, and sexy. Something had just clicked when he'd seen her, as if he'd been waiting for her.

When he got home, Lacey was waiting for him in the doorway. "What have you done?" she scolded. Hands on her hips, she blocked the doorway.

He walked up to her, picked her up, and set her aside. "I've just driven home, and now I'm going to go up and take a shower since I'm sweaty and have paint all over." He started up the stairs when Lacey darted in front of him again. One thing you had to say about her, she was fast.

When she blocked his path, he was tempted to set her aside again. She was three steps ahead of him, and they stood eye to eye. This time he could see the concern in her face. He stopped on the steps and sat down right there. Lacey sat next to him and put her hand on his arm. "Todd, I'm concerned for her. She needs time."

"I thought that too, but things just happened and…I'm not sorry. I love her. Actually, I think I've loved her for a long time. I know that sounds funny, but there you have it." He shrugged.

"You're serious?" Lacey stopped and thought a minute, while they sat on the steps. "How does she feel?"

"I'm not sure. Lacey, I know things are moving fast, but I'm tired of waiting. I know she's the one; I knew the first time I saw her." He looked into his sister's eyes and saw the understanding.

"Here's some advice. You may know it, but Megan needs time to understand it. Think of what she's coming from. Give her time to adjust." Lacey stood and gave him a quick kiss and hug.

Chapter Twelve

The next day was a busy one. The men had started installing the appliances before sunrise. Megan had them install all the appliances before they got started on the hot tub. There was problem after problem. First, the electricity for the honeymoon cabin had been wired wrong for the microwave. Then, when the electrician was wiring up for the hot tub, the breaker in the main house flipped, delaying the installation for the hot tub for an hour while he made another run to town to get a forty-amp breaker instead of a thirty.

By the time Megan headed up to get ready to go to Todd's, she had a full-blown headache.

But all the appliances were now installed, and they looked really good. The workers had filled up the hot tub and set the temperature to a toasty one hundred degrees. By tomorrow night, she'd be relaxing in it.

Matt had picked out oversized garden tubs, new toilets, and sinks for the cabin bathrooms, as well as stainless steel kitchen sinks and refrigerators. Things were definitely coming together.

She could have the furniture delivered early next week after she finished staining and sealing the floors, which she planned on doing after her cast was removed. She'd called the doctor and set an appointment to have it removed first thing in the morning.

But what had really capped the day off was the call from her lawyer about Derek. He said they were transferring him to a minimum-security facility at the end of the next month to await his trial, which had been moved back for the third time. Now it was set to take place in just under two months. He assured her this was a standard procedure and the trial would go smoothly.

She'd lived almost a year without Derek in her life full time, yet somehow she felt she'd never really be rid of his influence.

She had lain awake last night remembering the time spent with Todd and how different this was from any other relationship she'd ever had. She knew things couldn't get serious between them; she wasn't ready for that. But she would take what time she could with him and enjoy it.

Now she drove down the road to his house, looking forward to seeing him again. The road turned and then came into a clearing, where she stopped her car. Ahead of her was the house, though "manor" more accurately described it.

It was a huge stone two-story house with about twenty windows on the front. Lights came from about half of the lower windows. She'd been over here twice before, but the house looked bigger each time. The circular driveway went right up to the front door. Todd's and Lacey's cars sat out front. Megan pulled up beside them and parked.

When she got out of the Jeep, Bernard, Lacey's yellow lab, walked over and sniffed her feet. She'd seen him around several times before. He liked to hang out down by the beach or over by the pond. Megan bent and scratched him between the ears.

"What a fierce guard dog you are, Bernard," she whispered to him. He looked up at her and licked her hand, and she could have sworn he smiled back at her.

When she rang the doorbell, Bernard let out a loud bark, causing Megan to jump, and then he promptly sat at her feet.

Later that evening, everyone gathered on the patio out back. While Iian and Todd playfully argued over how to cook the steaks, Lacey chatted with her as they drank iced tea, and Bernard lay at her feet. The steaks, cooked to perfection, were served with grilled vegetables and grilled garlic bread.

After dinner, everyone sat around the fire in the living room, laughing and telling tales. Megan had never felt so much a part of something in her entire life. While they were chatting about food ideas for the bed-and-breakfast, the phone rang, and Lacey sprang up to answered it.

"Todd, it's that detective friend of yours from New York," Lacey called from the kitchen. Todd glanced at Megan with a guilty look and then went in to take the call.

The room was silent as he talked in the other room. She couldn't overhear anything, but she could feel the tension in the room.

Abruptly, she stood. "I'd better be going. It's been a long day."

Lacey walked her to the door. "I'm sure Todd will be off the phone in a minute."

"That's okay. I'll just…" Whatever she wanted to say died away as Todd came out of the kitchen. When he saw she had her hand on the doorknob, her coat in hand, he walked over to her.

"Are you leaving?" he asked, helping her with her coat.

"Yes," Megan said, pulling away from his touch.

He looked between Lacey and Megan, then gently took her arm and walked her outside. "What's this all about?" he asked when they were a safe distance from the house.

"Why do you need a detective in New York?" Megan asked in a harsh tone. All of a sudden, she felt chilled. Her light jacket seemed to let all the warmth from her body escape.

"He was checking up on a few loose ends," Todd said, trying to reach for her again. Megan jerked away so fast she almost stumbled.

"Does it have anything to do with me?" she bit out.

"Yes," was all he said.

"Good night." She stalked to her car.

She would have made it, but Todd was too fast. He grabbed her by the shoulders and spun her around. "What is this all about? I hired someone to check up on your ex-husband. Not you."

"You're hurting me," Megan whispered and looked down at his hands, which were flexing on her shoulders. She didn't mean physically but didn't want to explain her emotional pain just then. "How could you?" she asked quietly.

Todd released her shoulders and shoved his hands into his pockets. “I wanted to make sure he was put away.”

“I don’t need a protector, Todd. I can look out for myself. I don’t need someone to check up on me. God!” she said, throwing up her hand. “This is why I never told Matt anything. I’m not looking for a knight to come charging in and make everything bad disappear.” Megan began rubbing her hands together.

“I won’t apologize for wanting to make sure you’re safe, Megan,” Todd said in a low voice.

“I can take care of myself, Todd,” she said again, but it came out as a whisper.

“Yes, I can see that. You’ve done a smashing job so far.” The sarcasm rolled off him, hitting her full force.

Megan took a breath to recover the blow.

“I don’t like people going behind my back. I don’t need someone else running my life,” she said and got into her car.

Todd let her go. He knew he’d overstepped his bounds, but he was only trying to protect her.

Couldn't she see that? She was small and he hadn't meant to hurt her. He'd instantly regretted his words but felt they needed to be said. After all, if someone had been there to help her before, he was sure she wouldn't have had to go through so much pain.

He was in a sour mood now and knew it would be a long time before he could settle down, so he stalked to the barn to see Chester.

As Megan drove home, her temper didn't improve. She kept running what he'd said over and over in her mind. Why did people always treat her like she was some helpless child? When her coworkers had learned she was having marital problems, they'd all treated her like she was some ignorant child who couldn't tie her own shoes. She kept her life private; that was the way she liked it. If someone wanted to know something about her, all they had to do was ask. That way, she could give them the answer she wanted them to hear.

Why did Todd want to control her like this? She wanted to start a new life, and that meant not being controlled by anyone. By the time she got home and slammed the front door, she'd talked herself into a terrible frenzy. She paced around the house, mumbling to herself.

An hour later, she still couldn't quite settle down. She sat at her desk to work on some paperwork she'd been putting off, but she couldn't focus. Her mind kept replaying little things Derek had done, like checking up on her every move or calling her while she was driving and staying on the phone until he knew she was in her office, just to make sure she didn't stop anywhere for a quick affair. Sometimes he would call her office and demand to speak to her, accusing her of having an in-office affair if she was unavailable to talk.

She was so preoccupied by running through the memories that by the time she looked up from the computer, it was four o'clock in the morning. Her eyes were dry and scratchy and her neck hurt. Leaving the computer running, she walked upstairs, collapsed into bed with her clothes on, and fell asleep the moment her head hit the pillow.

When she woke, it was to pounding. She blinked and sat up, then realized it was someone at the front door.

After stumbling out of bed, she headed down the stairs. When she reached the bottom, she heard Todd calling her name over and over. She opened the door just as he was going to pound again.

He barged in and, looking around, demanded, "Are you all right? Are you hurt? What's happened?"

"What?" She ran a hand through her hair, trying to get her bearings. "What are you talking about?"

Todd took a step back. "I've been knocking on your door for about five minutes. I was about to run home and get my set of keys or break down the door."

She knew her hair was a mess and her eyes probably had purple lines under them. She'd even slept in the clothes she'd worn last night.

"What are you doing here, Todd?" She leaned against the door.

"Your doctor's appointment. You do want to get that cast removed today, right?"

"Oh, yes." She perked up a little. "Let me go freshen up." She quickly disappeared upstairs.

When Megan came back down five minutes later, she had on a clean pair of slacks and a blue blouse, and her hair hung in a long, straight ponytail. She was looking forward to being able to do more with it once her cast was removed.

When she walked into her office, she stopped short. When she'd left her office last night, papers had been piled all over the desk and the computer screen had still been on. Now, however, Todd sat behind the desk looking over the paperwork. He had all the bills in a neat stack and the desk was clean of clutter. All the hurt and anger from the night before surfaced again.

A memory flashed in her mind of Derek sitting behind a desk, handing her twenty dollars for gas and lunch. He'd never allowed her access to any of her money.

"What are you doing?" she asked, walking into the room while trying to control the shaking in her hands.

Todd looked up. When he started to speak, Megan picked up the stack of papers.

"Don't," she said, and then tossed them in the air, letting them float down all over the desk and floor.

Todd's mouth dropped open, and he blinked at her. "I can drive myself to the damn doctor," she said and walked out.

Todd sat behind the desk for another thirty seconds before his mind went into action. He caught her at the front door. Placing his hand on the door over her shoulder, he kept her from storming out.

"Megan, I'm sorry," he said to her back. "I shouldn't have interfered. I'm used to coming and going, and well…there's no excuse for my rudeness." He reached down and lightly took her hand, turning her around. "Please, let's not fight." He ran a finger down her cheek. "I only wanted to help."

"I'm used to everyone treating me like a child. I can do my own finances and clean up after myself. I can take care of myself. I don't want to be controlled or treated that way again. Can you understand?" she said, pulling her hand away.

"It won't happen again. Trust me, I know you're not a child." He smiled down at her.

"I—I need some time. I thought I was ready for this. But I don't know what I want now." She looked back up at him. "Can you give me some time to sort things out?"

He hesitated. "Are you sorry, then?"

"No!" she said a little too urgently. "I think I just need some time…" She drifted off.

"Time?" Todd saw something other than fear in her eyes. He knew he was rushing things with her, but he wanted her in his life for good. But he didn't want to scare her off. If he truly wanted her in his life, then he could be patient. "Sure, come on, let's get this cast off. We're running a little late, and Dr. Stevens is a stickler about punctuality."

She nodded. He helped her into her jacket, and they set off.

It was a cool spring morning, and she could smell moisture in the air. She'd learned it meant it would be a wet evening. Her arm hurt whenever it rained, as did all the other bones that had been broken. She thought about taking some Tylenol when she got home.

She really did enjoy the feel of a small town. She'd always lived in the city, and this was completely different from anything she'd experienced before.

Every time she went to town, she met new people, talking for hours at a time. Getting to know the history of the town and the people was nice. As they drove down the two-lane street that went straight into the center of town, almost everyone stopped and waved.

Several of the church ladies gathered outside the market. Megan waved, and they all stopped talking and waved back. When they drove by, she could see their heads coming together in fast gossip.

Megan looked over at Todd and realized it would be all over town that they were going somewhere together. She was sure that when they got out of the car at the other end of the block, she could hear their names on the wind, and she glanced back over towards the bunch. The women's heads quickly turned away, back to a huddle.

"Don't mind them." He took her arm and led her up the stairs. "Small towns have big mouths."

Dr. Stevens was a short, thin man who looked at least a hundred and three. When Megan first came into his office, she expected a secretary or at least a waiting room. Instead, they entered into a hallway and immediately to the right was a small office. Todd knocked on the open door and walked right in.

"Todd, my boy, come in, come in. This must be Megan," he said, standing up and holding out his left hand for a quick shake. He had thick gray hair and thin-rimmed glasses that slipped off his straight nose. "Well, come on back, my dear. Todd, you can wait here." He pointed to an old blue couch. Todd smiled and gladly sat down.

Dr. Stevens showed her down the hall to the first dressing room. "You have a seat in here." He patted the table. She hopped up on it, letting her legs swing. She felt like a small child all over again. She'd had plenty of trips to the doctor after her parents' death, and plenty of hospital visits due to Derek. Doctors and hospitals always made her nervous. She didn't like explaining things, and doctors and nurses tended to ask a lot of questions.

"I hear we're taking this thing off today," he said, looking at the cast. "Shouldn't be too bad. Anything else? How are you physically? When was your last exam?" he asked, pulling out a chart and sitting at the small table.

"Oh, well. I had a complete physical before I left Boston. I'm feeling fine, just the cast."

He wrote a few things down in the folder. "Because you can't fill out these forms here, I'll do it for you. Will you be living here, then?" he asked, glancing over his shoulder.

"Um, yes," she said, softly.

"Good, good. Who was your doctor in Boston?"

Megan listed off the doctor who had last examined her, handed over her insurance card, and finished answering basic questions. She noted that not once did the old man ask how she had broken her arm or any other personal questions. She liked him for that.

Todd sat in Dr. Steven's office and looked around. The site was very familiar, as was the smell. It had been a while since he'd needed to sit here.

He remembered waiting for Sara during one of her many exams and thinking their kids would grow up being treated in this same office. Dr. Stevens would still be behind his desk.

As the sadness grew, a faint hope came into view. Megan walked in the door holding her right arm, which was bare, cleaned, and looking smaller and paler than the other one. She had a smile on her face and a sucker in her mouth.

"I always wanted a doctor who gave out suckers. You don't get that in the city," she said, twirling the sucker and smiling at Dr. Stevens, who walked in and sat back at his desk.

"I know you had an exam in Boston, but when your paperwork gets here, I'd like to see you again," he said, writing something down in her file. "Now take it easy, no heavy lifting with that arm. You might want to take some aspirin when you get home for any pain. I'll give you a call when your files come in. Still using Matt's number?" When Megan nodded, he continued. "Good, we'll see you then."

Then he looked over at Todd. "Todd, my boy, I was going through my files, and it appears you need to renew your tetanus shot. Would you like to take care of that today?"

The color drained from his face at the thought of getting a shot. "Um," he started to say.

Before he could answer, Dr. Stevens said, "Good. Come on back." Then he disappeared through the door again.

"Like I said, good doctor," Todd mumbled, walking out the door with his head held low and Megan laughing at his back.

Spring was finally in full swing, and the next days were relatively busy. Every time she turned around, it seemed there was someone stopping by.

The photographer, Brad Stone, had dropped by one sunny day and taken loads of pictures. He was an older man in his mid-fifties with a full beard that was snow white. They looked at the pictures on her computer and e-mailed the best ones to the website designer. Brad had promised her prints of them in the mail for the fliers and brochures she was going to have printed.

The cabins were finished, and Megan had begun decorating. The furniture Matt had ordered was perfect.

She'd gone shopping with Allison and Lacey in Portland one day, getting everything from trashcans to bed linens. They'd even purchased shower curtains, towels, and window coverings for all the cabins. Everything matched what she had envisioned in each cabin. She enjoyed putting the small touches in each room with Lacey's and Allison's help.

Allison had dropped by several days in a row to sit and paint each of the cabins and the main house. She wouldn't let Megan see them until she had finished them all. When she was done, there were small paintings of each cabin and a larger one of the house, each of them better than Megan could have hoped for. Allison promised to return each one framed.

She had planted flowers in the beds around the house, along the trail, and around the cabins, and they were all blooming beautifully. She had also taken some time to plant a small garden below the deck off her own bedroom, so when she stepped out, she could see her vegetables growing.

Her arm grew stronger every day and she forced herself not to pamper it too much. She enjoyed her daily walks to the cabins and most days made the extra trek to the beach. Most of all, she enjoyed having time to herself to do what she wanted, when she wanted.

While she was working hard in her garden trying to tackle the weeds one evening, a small black Audi bumped up her driveway. Her smile widened when she saw Ric emerge.

"Hi," she called from the side of the house, shielding her eyes from the sun.

"Good evening." He came over to her. "You have a lovely spot here," he said, looking around. "I thought I would stop by after my meeting with Allison."

Megan set down the small spade she'd been holding. "Let me pour you some tea, and you can tell me all about it." She motioned for him to follow her to the front porch, where a cool pitcher and glasses sat on the table.

"It went very well," he said, taking the glass she offered. "She signed on with an agent, and I have a box load of paintings she'll be shipping to me first thing tomorrow. I wanted to come by and thank you personally. Allison is a great find. I owe you more than I can repay." He set the glass down on the table and picked up her hand, holding it in his. "Let me show you by taking you out to dinner tonight."

"Oh, that's really not necessary," she began.

"Please, I wanted to talk with you further about the possibility of you helping me out some more."

"Um, well…"

"Good," he jumped in without waiting for her answer. "Now, where is a good place to eat around here?"

Half an hour later, Megan was seated at a small table for two facing the water at the Golden Oar. Ric sat across the dimly lit table, his attention momentarily diverted to the artwork. Megan could see the desire in his eyes, and then he blinked it away and smiled at her.

"What's good here?" he asked, picking up his menu.

"Everything. Todd's family owns this place. Iian and Lacey, Todd's brother and sister, run it. Iian is an excellent chef." Just then, a small, stout waitress came over to take their orders.

How could she do this to him? Hadn't he shown her patience? Hadn't he taken a step back? Hadn't he made it clear to her he was hers? He looked out the small window in the kitchen door and stared at the back of a man's head, a man who reached over to hold Megan's hand. He wanted to tear someone apart, and why not start with the blond man sitting across the room? Opening the door a little harder than necessary, he began to cross the room.

When he was about halfway to the table, Megan spotted him. She pulled her hand out of Ric's as he stopped at the table. Seeing him, Ric stood and stretched out his hand to shake.

"Good evening, Todd. Megan and I were just having dinner and discussing some business. Would you care to join us?" Ric said smoothly. Without giving Todd time to answer, Ric turned and motioned for a waitress to bring another chair. "She was telling me your family owns this lovely establishment," he continued after they all sat back down. Todd still felt frustrated. "I would love to know more about that lovely creature." He pointed towards the canvas that displayed the mermaid.

Before answering, Todd reached over and took Megan's hand in his own. It was cold, and he could see a lost look in her eyes. He hadn't meant to scare her. Rubbing his thumb over her cold flesh, he gave Ric an empty smile and answered. "The Golden Oar has been in our family for generations. All the art in here is my grandmother's work." Todd looked around, a wave of pride flowing through him.

"It's exquisite work. I would love to get my hands on some of it." Ric sat back down. "I've just come from meeting with Allison. We're trying to set up a showing in my Los Angeles gallery next month," Ric said over a cup of coffee. "I offered Allison the apartment above my gallery in Los Angeles. It will be nice to have someone staying there instead of the place collecting dust. It couldn't hurt her work to have more experience and travel."

"Allison's moving?" Megan sat straighter in her chair at this news.

"She's giving it some thought. Her mother wants to sell the store and Allison wants to spread her wings. Her words, not mine," Ric said.

An hour later, their laughter could be heard throughout the restaurant. Ric and Todd become fast friends, and Todd could tell that Megan was more relaxed sitting next to him.

The evening ended on a high note. Todd drove Megan home, and they sat on the porch swing watching the sun set.

"Have you ever been sailing?" Todd asked, running his hand over her hair.

"No. Do you sail?" she asked, leaning into his shoulder.

"Yes, how about tomorrow?" he asked with a smile and leaned in for a quick kiss.

She was nervous for the first half hour out on the water, but after he let her take the helm, she relaxed and enjoyed the feel of the wind on her face.

He told her that he would make sure to stay within sight of land. He showed her a group of sea lions sunbathing on some rocks near the point.

They stayed out on the water until after the sun went down and they could see all the lights of town turning on. They sat a ways out from the shore and enjoyed a picnic dinner with the full moon overhead and the town lights twinkling in the distance. She'd never enjoyed a more relaxing and romantic day.

She could tell he was making a point not to pressure her. He kissed her on her front porch when he dropped her off at home for the evening. The next day, he sent a small bouquet of flowers with a note thanking her for a wonderful time and saying he couldn't wait to see her again.

Even when the evenings started getting warmer, it was cool enough that she'd taken to using the hot tub almost every night to relax. She still had trouble sleeping through the night and found a small glass of wine helped her sleep better, not to mention that it helped her sore back.

She thought about building an overhang on the deck so that when winter came, she could sit out in the tub and enjoy the snow.

Todd had had little opportunity over the last few weeks, but he finally found time to swing by the cemetery and visit Matt. The rain that day had yet to let up, and he'd forgotten his raincoat. He hunched over the black tombstone of his best friend, holding his sister's bright green umbrella.

Todd had been trying to slowly reach out to Megan, to make her more comfortable around him again. He felt like such a failure at showing her the kindness she deserved. One thing was for sure—he still felt justified in looking into her ex, but he never brought up the subject with her.

"Well, Matt, I don't know if you're watching over us, but I hope you're okay with Megan and me. I didn't expect to find her, to feel this way about her. She went through hell, and I mean to show her things can be good, and if it's all right with you…" He waited a beat, listening for…something, anything. "I love her more than I can stand. I mean to marry her, and I hope to God you're good with that."

When Megan woke up, it was to the sound of thunder. She knew she wouldn't get any outside work done, so she settled in to complete some of the paperwork she'd been putting off.

About halfway through balancing her checkbook, she heard a loud boom from the back of the house.

The storm continued to rage outside. It had been lightning and thundering for about half an hour now. Thinking the noise must be a tree branch hitting the house, she ignored it, but when it continued, she got up and walked through the house to the back door. Looking out the window, she couldn't see anything except rain streaming down the glass.

When she turned her back on the door, she heard it again. *Boom, boom, boom.* Three in a row. It sounded like it was coming from something hitting the door. She reached over and grabbed the nearest item as a weapon. Fumbling for the handle, she unlocked the dead bolt and slowly opened the door. When she had it open a few inches, something large and black darted in the door and ran under the kitchen table.

Megan let out a quick yelp and slammed the door shut, jumping again when lightning flashed and she caught her reflection in the glass doors. Calming herself, she looked down at the wooden spoon she held as a weapon. Tossing it into the sink, she grabbed up her broom and slowly walked to the table.

"Okay," she said to herself and the animal now hiding under her table. "A cat or a rabbit, maybe a squirrel or some other harmless animal. Please let it be a cat."

She could see wet paw prints on the floor and could hear a low moan. It had looked bigger than any cat she'd ever seen. She was thinking a raccoon. *Please don't be a raccoon.* Did they have raccoons here? Was it a skunk? She'd seen black and white, but the thing was so wet, it was hard to tell what it was.

She slowly reached for the tablecloth, pulling it up a few inches. Just then, there was a loud boom from outside, and the lights went out.

"Great! Just great! There's a wild animal in my house, and now I have no lights." She made her way through the dark to the cabinets and fumbled around in the drawer until she found the flashlight. She clicked the button and breathed a sigh of relief when the white beam swept across the room.

Slowly going over to the table, she pulled up the tablecloth more quickly than she should have. From below the table, she heard a loud hiss. “Okay, that rules out a skunk, I think. You must be a cat.” She pointed the light at its green eyes. It huddled in the corner farthest from her and hissed again when the light shone on it.

“Well, if you had knocked nicely, I would have let you in. You must be cold, poor thing.” Leaving the tablecloth up, she went over to the refrigerator and pulled out the milk. “I’m afraid I only drink two percent, but I bet you don’t mind.” She pulled out a bowl and poured milk into it. Setting the bowl down, she sat next to it on the cold floor. She grabbed the hand towel off the oven and put it in her lap.

It took about one minute for the animal to crawl out from under the table and scamper over to the bowl. It started quickly lapping up the milk. It was bigger than most cats, but it was rail thin, its hair matted and soaked through.

Slowly she reached over and started to pet it. The cat looked up briefly and then continued to lap up the milk.

Megan reached down and started rubbing its hair dry. When the milk was gone, it began purring loudly. Then it came over, climbed up on her lap, and started to bathe itself.

"Well, I guess I could use a mouser around here," she said, looking into the cat's eyes. It had no collar or tags on. "Because I don't know if you're a female or male, and I don't think it would be very nice of me to check, seeing as we just met, how about I call you Boomer?" she asked, scratching its head.

The cat gave a loud meow and head butted her, rubbing its face against hers, all the while continuing to purr.

The lights flashed back on and the cat flicked its tail and walked off, starting to explore the room. Megan made a mental note to ask Todd if there was a good veterinarian in town. She would also have to get cat food and a litter box.

She'd been enjoying the quiet of the house, but she did feel lonely. She was glad she now had someone to talk to. As she went back towards her office, the cat bounced along with her, running between her legs and flicking its tail.

Megan chatted to Boomer about the house and anything else she thought of. She sat at the desk, and the cat jumped up on the couch and looked across the room at her. Five minutes later, it was fast asleep, curled up in a tight black ball. The storm continued all evening. She was making some chicken noodle soup for herself and Boomer when she heard a car drive up.

Looking out the window, she saw Todd's car park by the garage and a dark figure sprint for the back door. She knew he would let himself in, so she continued stirring the soup with the cat sitting at her feet.

"Well, what do we have here?" Todd asked, shaking the rain from his hair by the doorway.

Megan glanced over her shoulder. "You're right in time for dinner," she said, going over and pulling out another bowl. There was French bread heating up in the oven, making the house smell good. "This is Boomer. Boomer, this is Todd," Megan said, pouring soup into the bowls.

Todd came over and scratched Boomer's neck and kissed Megan on the cheek. "Where did you find this fellow?" he asked, pulling a bottle of wine from the refrigerator and pouring them each a glass.

"He found me. Came knocking on my door. He said it was too wet outside and he wanted to come live with me, to keep me company, oh, and to eat all my mice," she said, smiling.

"He did, did he? Well, I guess that seems like a fair trade. You keep him dry, and he eats mice." He came up behind her and put his hands around her, and she noticed that she didn't even flinch at his touch.

"He hasn't left my side since he came running into the house. You don't know if he belongs to anyone around here, do you?" she asked as they sat at the table.

"No, the Bells are down the road a ways, and they have dogs, not cats. I think maybe he was a barn cat. He's well behaved, though, and huge. A little thin, but I'm sure you can fix that," Todd said when the cat finished the whole bowl of soup and then lay down on the floor to bathe itself. "I came over to tell you, I have to go out of town for about a week. I'm heading to California for some meetings." He looked over the table at her, pulling her hand into his. "I really wanted to see you before I left tomorrow."

Although Todd's daily visits were great, a reprieve would be nice. She didn't want to become too attached. It scared her how much she felt for him. She'd asked for time and space, but secretly she wanted to spend every minute with him. She wanted to fall asleep in his arms and wake up in them as well. She wanted him day and night. She wanted him now.

They finished their soup, and she got up to take the bowls to the sink, but something stopped her. Her hand hovered above his bowl and she thought about being with him. About how he treated her, how he was kind and patient, something she'd only experienced with her brother before. Todd sat very still. His hands were on the table with his fingers spread out, his eyes on hers. Deciding to take a chance at life, she set her bowl back down on the table, and as he moved his hands, she straddled him, her legs on either side of his, caging him in.

"I want you," she whispered. "I can't stop wanting you."

She lost all ability to think when she was this close to him. Her inner thigh muscles contracted around him, and all of a sudden, she was kissing him. As the kiss grew deeper, her hands roamed all over him and his hands finally left the table to grab hold of her waist. He tightened his grip, digging into her hips, pulling her closer. Her breasts pushed against his chest. She wanted him more then she'd ever wanted anyone before.

"Are you sure? Make sure, Megan, because if you tell me to leave now, I'll go…Don't tell me to go," he whispered.

"Stay, please stay." Megan fisted her hands in his hair, pulling his face back to hers.

The feel of him, the smell of him made her go crazy. He pushed up from the chair, taking her along. She wrapped her legs around his waist and held on. He marched them towards the stairs and was up them in record time. When he struggled to open the door, she helped him push it open. Once inside, she arched away and took off her shirt. She tossed it to the ground and their mouths came back together. Then she hit the bed with a small bounce and a laugh. A second later, Todd's body covered hers. She reached to untuck his shirt, to touch the skin beneath. His stomach muscles bunched under her fingers as she pulled his shirt over his head, wanting to feel more.

Everywhere his skin touched hers, she burned, and she couldn't get enough. He made a trail of kisses down her throat, using his tongue and teeth to send shivers down her entire body.

At times, she thought she would go crazy with wanting him. Now that she was finally underneath him again, she felt that he couldn't go fast or slow enough. His hands shook as he reached to remove her pants, so she helped him remove them, and then reached for his.

He took her hands. "Let me just touch you," he said, putting her hands above her head so that she was exposed for him. She had a white camisole on, and he played with the strings, holding it up. His fingers slowly wandered down to the taut nipple. She let out a moan when he pinched it lightly through the thin material. He looked back up at her face. Her hair was messed up, loose as his hands played with it. Her cheeks turned pink and flushed as her eyes closed and her mouth opened slightly. He started kissing her lightly. He was confusing her, and she was enjoying it. She thought she wanted speed, but found that him driving her crazy with slowness did the same.

He kept her hands locked above her head with one of his in a light grip as he explored her. She could have broken loose if she tried, but she didn't. Pulling the camisole down, he took her into his mouth, nibbling on her nipple, which stood erect for him to play with. His fingers moved lower to play with the top of the white lace that covered the triangle of soft hair.

He tortured her lightly with his fingers while his mouth grew stronger, sucking and tugging. His hand slid down slowly towards her heat, playing with her through the thin lace. He could feel her wetness, and, pressing lightly, he rubbed the soft material against her.

His mouth paused and then began a journey down to replace his hand, his tongue taking the place of his fingers on the lace. He smelled her sweet arousal and almost lost control.

Slowly, he let his finger slide underneath the elastic to enjoy the soft folds, while his tongue lapped at the lace. And just when he thought he couldn't wait any longer, he pulled aside the lace and put his mouth to her, again using his tongue to heat her. She tasted of spring; he couldn't get enough. She pushed her legs apart with his hands and tugged the lace aside, holding her wide open for his exploration. He nibbled lightly on the bud and pushed his tongue far into her core, moaning when a fresh wave of sweet heat hit his mouth.

She moaned and gripped his hair in her hands, holding him down. In a swift move, he slid the lace down her silky legs, pushing them wider. He was tasting, probing, until she squirmed and tugged on his head.

"Todd, now, please, now," she moaned. He quickly discarded his jeans and then he pushed up and in one swift move embedded himself in her heat as she screamed his name, her nails digging into his shoulders.

His lungs felt like they were on fire, his body screamed for release, but he held off, waiting for her. She had wrapped her legs around his hips and was trying to pull him closer while her back came off the bed. He gripped her hips, placing one hand on her lower back, her legs holding her to him. He reached down between them as her legs held her in place. The slightest touch was all it took. She exploded in one swift movement, and he joined her.

Even if the house were on fire, he wouldn't have been able to move a muscle. His weight pinned her to the mattress, and her hands fell limply by his sides. His breath heated her neck as he buried his face in her hair. This was where he wanted to stay all night, just like this. He started to move aside, but she grabbed him. "No, stay."

"I've got to be crushing you," he murmured into her hair.

"No, you're very skinny." Reaching around, she grabbed his butt. "And I like it just like this," she said in a dreamy voice that was huskier than normal.

His mind spun. The way he saw it, he had two choices. He could move in here and they could get married by Christmas, or he could take her with him tomorrow, and they could swing through Vegas on the way home. He liked the second idea better. He just needed to convince her. Rolling onto his back, he pulled up the blankets and pulled her closer, her head resting on his chest and her hair fanned out over his shoulder.

She sighed and settled in as he kissed her head and closed his eyes and took a deep breath. Sometimes it was better not to overthink things.

"Marry me," he blurted out, keeping his eyes tightly shut.

Chapter Thirteen

He had expected her to be…Well, he didn't know what he'd expected, but it sure wasn't what he got.

She tensed and then sat straight up, pulling the covers with her. He wanted to see her face, but she had turned away from him. Then she quickly jumped out of bed. Not saying a word, she pulled the sheets with her and went into the bathroom, shutting the door just as he sat up in bed.

Walking over to the bathroom door, he could hear her putting on clothes. As he was about to knock, she yanked open the door.

"Don't," she said, holding up her hands. She'd put on an oversized T-shirt, one of Matt's. It hit her mid-thigh, leaving her legs bare. “Why can’t we just stay like this?”

He stood there, naked. “Because I want it all with you,” he said, reaching for her.

She pulled aside and walked to the French doors, opening them wide and letting in the cool night air. Todd moved over and stood behind her, then pulled her into his arms. She tensed, so he pulled her closer, dipping his mouth to her neck.

“We’re good together, trust me. It doesn’t happen often that two people who were meant to be together find each other, Megan.”

Turning her around so that she faced him, he said, “I recognized you the first time I laid eyes on you. You’re for me, Megan.” Dipping his head, he claimed her mouth. The kiss was powerful, and it seared her. She tried to move away, but he held her firmly against his naked body. “Please, let me hold you.”

After a few seconds of silence, he walked them backward towards the bed, but she stopped him, placing her hands on his chest. “I can’t do this now, Todd. Can you understand? I need time. I-I don’t ever want to get married again, to belong to someone, like property. I won’t do that again, ever.” She pulled farther away, backing up several steps.

When she just stared at him, he leaned down slowly and claimed her mouth again, this time in a featherlight kiss. "I'll give you time to get used to it, but we belong together."

A few hours later, Megan lay beside Todd, their legs intertwined. The cat scampered in not long after they settled down and was now curled up on Todd's chest. Todd, oblivious to the fact, snored lightly, with Boomer's body rising and falling with each breath. If Megan hadn't been so lost in her thoughts, she would have laughed at the picture they made.

Marriage? Never! Or so she'd thought. Would marriage be different with Todd? What was she thinking? She'd known him for only about three months now. She'd known Derek for almost a full year prior to getting married. She knew people could hide things and usually did.

Would Todd be like that? Controlling, domineering, abusive? Everything inside her heart and head said no. His family was proof enough of that, and if she wanted additional proof, all she had to do was turn her head and take a look at the black cat purring between Todd's light snores. Derek had hated all animals. When they got married, he'd forced her to get rid of the small tabby she'd had since moving out on her own. The cat had always hissed at him when he came into a room.

As she lay there, her legs intertwined with his, she remembered the scene the first day Derek had told her to get rid of the cat.

"That cat obviously has issues. I mean, every time someone walks into a room, it goes crazy. Do you really want to have it go ape-shit every time we have people over? You know my job has expectations and I have responsibilities to the firm. Just get rid of it, or I will."

Back then, Megan would have done anything to please him. She had thought it was love, but she'd been so naive.

Turning her head now, she glanced over at Todd's silhouette. His mouth was slightly open, the cat comfortably snoring along. Todd had a great profile. Her gaze traveled from his straight forehead, down the bridge of his nose, which had a slight upward turn at the end that made her think of a small ski slope. She looked at his lips next. Remembering how they felt on her, she smiled and blushed slightly.

He had a strong chin. She liked looking at him. He was a lot easier on the eyes than Derek had ever been. Todd was tall and thin. Derek had a stocky build, with thinning blond hair. He'd been in good shape when they met but had quickly gained thirty pounds after the wedding. Todd would still look thin with an extra thirty pounds.

She reached over and scratched Boomer's ears and curled up to the pair, falling asleep to the soft snoring of man and beast.

Megan woke to a rich aroma drifting from the kitchen; she could get used to having someone cook for her. The cat snored comfortably on her stomach. She reached down and scratched his head, and he gave a quick yawn and stretched.

"Well, Boomer, I guess we better go see what Todd's cooking."

The cat let out a meow and jogged behind her into the kitchen. They ate French toast and eggs. Todd demanded that she go relax after breakfast, and he put away the dishes. She could definitely get used to this.

Walking into the living room, she took the photo album to the couch and started looking through one of Matt's old photo books.

"Are those your parents?" Todd asked over her shoulder. Megan jumped. She hadn't heard him approach from behind. "Sorry." He reached over and started lightly rubbing her shoulders. Leaning in, he placed a kiss on her neck.

"Yes," she said, glancing down at the old photo. It had to be the only family picture she'd ever seen. "I didn't know Matt had this. I've never seen it."

Todd walked around and sat next to her, looking down at the photo. "You look a lot like your mother. You and Matt have her eyes."

Megan smiled at this. "I can remember her singing to me at night." She leaned her head on his shoulder. "She would sing *Amazing Grace* or"—Megan chuckled—"*You Are My Sunshine*. I always asked for the sun song. I can't really remember my father. Is that bad?"

"No, not from what Matt told me about him. Sounds like your mother was a wonderful woman, though. Matt never told me exactly how they died, only that they both went at the same time, and that's when he gained custody of you. I think he was… what? Nineteen? One of the reasons we became so close was that we had both lost our parents and had family that needed us."

"Nineteen, a very young age for a boy to become father and mother rolled into one." Megan took a deep breath. "My father killed her and then tried to strangle me. I guess he couldn't do it, though. He shot himself before the neighbors found me, bruised, half-naked, walking through the streets. He was always very possessive and controlling. She was trying to leave him."

Todd didn't say anything; he gripped her hand.

Megan smiled to herself. "I loved her very much when I was little, and I wanted to grow up to be just like her. I guess I did, in more ways than I wanted."

"Don't. You've had some bad luck with men, until now." Todd turned her to face him and set the book down. "I'll never hurt you. That's my promise to you, Megan. I've never raised a hand to a woman, and I never will. I'm not saying we'll always get along. I'm smarter than that. I know relationships take twists and turns, but I can promise you this—I'll never hurt you."

Megan leaned her forehead against his. "I know. I trust you completely, and it scares me, but now…"

Todd reached up and pulled her face to his. The kiss was light and soothed Megan's tortured mind. An image of this scene years from now flashed in her mind. She could see them sitting before a fire, older, with kids running around the house. Letting out a sigh, she kissed him back with something that had been building up inside her.

When their lips parted, he whispered, "Let me take you upstairs." He pulled closer and started to pick her up.

"Don't you have a plane to catch?" she teased.

"There's always another one," he said between kisses.

"No, you need to get going. There will be time when you get home." She pulled away, dodging his lips, and laughed at the face he made at her.

Megan kept herself busy the next few days. Todd had left on his trip with a promise to call every day, and he did. She kept telling herself she didn't miss him, but every time she turned around, she thought about him.

She was sitting at her desk, running over some ad ideas, when the phone rang. When she hung up five minutes later, she was jumping around, laughing. She had her first customers! She had booked a family for three nights starting this weekend. Then, as it hit her—this weekend!—she promptly sat back down.

There was so much left to do, and she hadn't figured out yet how to work the billing software Iian had installed on her computer. She had the meals planned but hadn't yet printed up a list to place in each of the cabins. There was the matter of stocking the refrigerators, and many more odds and ends that came to mind.

She quickly made a list and then called Lacey to see if she could come over the next day to help. By the time she went to bed that night, her stomach was in knots. It seemed like so many things still needed to be done, and there were only two days to get them completed.

She headed upstairs and decided it would be a perfect night to sit in the hot tub and try to relax.

Boomer sat at the edge and looked like he wanted to join her. She really enjoyed his company.

The day after she'd found him, she'd picked up cat food and a litter box and had purchased every type of cat toy the store had in stock. He even had a new scratching post in the corner of her room. He was a spoiled cat. In the few days he'd been there, she could see he'd already gained some weight. She had, of course, taken him to the vet the next day as well. Boomer was a boy. He was now up to date on shots and wore a collar and a shiny tag with his name and address on it.

The vet said he thought Boomer was about two years old. He could stand to gain some weight, but now that he was in a loving home, she didn't think that would be a problem.

When Megan got out of the hot tub, Boomer jumped up on the bed, curled up on the pillow Todd had used, and quickly fell asleep. This had been their routine; she liked having a routine and having someone to share it with.

The next morning, she woke up late. Her body ached, and when she stood up, she had to run to the restroom, where she immediately got sick. She had a slight temperature and took a couple of aspirin before heading downstairs.

When Lacey arrived an hour later, she almost dropped the box of cinnamon rolls she was holding.

"What's wrong? Are you sick?" she said, walking Megan to the couch while feeling her forehead. "You've got a fever. Did you take anything?"

"Yes, a couple of aspirin." Megan let Lacey push her down on the couch and put her feet up.

"Aspirin, good. I'll go make you some soup. You rest now." Lacey rushed out.

Megan tried, but her head and stomach were spinning. By the time the smell of the soup filled the house, she was back in the bathroom. She started feeling a little better by noon but still spent the day on the couch.

"The aspirin took care of most of the aches. I still feel run down, though," she told Lacey.

"There was a twenty-four-hour bug going around town. I had it last week, myself," Lacey said.

They worked until late that evening to finish everything on her list. Lacey really helped out. She printed the menus on card stock and placed them in silver frames Megan had purchased from Allison's store. Everything was ready for her first customers.

She had shipped her printed brochures to Ric and delivered some to each of the stores in town the week before. They had a beautiful color picture of the honeymoon cabin on the cover and had turned out exactly as she had hoped.

"Todd asked me to marry him," Megan said later on. They'd decided to celebrate the official opening of Pride Bed-and-Breakfast over the cinnamon rolls.

"And?" Lacey asked. She sat on the end of the couch with a cup of hot chocolate in her hands.

"You don't seem surprised." Megan looked over at her.

"I've seen the way he looks at you. Todd isn't one to mess around. When he wants something, he usually gets it." She smiled at Megan.

"I don't know what to do. I didn't give him an answer. I need some time to figure my life out. There's so much that I want to…I don't know."

"You need to find yourself first," Lacey said plainly, giving Megan a look of understanding. "You know about Todd's past?" When Megan nodded, she continued. "Todd wasn't really in love with Sara. I mean, there was a time when he was. But I think it was more love out of obligation than anything. Sara had been raised by her father; her mother died when she was young. Her father was the town drunk, and he neglected Sara altogether. I remember seeing her in the store one day. She had gotten a job there when she was fourteen. After her mother died, her father refused to acknowledge her. It was almost as if Sara didn't exist in his eyes. She had to fend for herself, buying food, clothing, and everything. I think she could have dealt with it better if he'd hit her, but to have someone you love just…ignore you." Lacey shook her head. "When Todd and Sara graduated school, she moved into the apartment above the store, and Todd went away to school out east. After a year, though, he moved back, and they married." Megan couldn't imagine being ignored. There'd been times in her life when she'd wished she *had* been ignored.

Boomer jumped up on the couch and lay down on Lacey's lap. Lacey scratched his neck, smiling when he rolled over so she could do the same to his stomach. "I can see how he feels for you. It's right there on his face whenever he talks about you or looks at you. I know you want to start your life over here. Take the time to think about all your options. The answers will come to you."

"I have these feelings for Todd. I've never felt like this before, for anyone. I can't explain them or how they make me feel. All I know is they scare me. I wish I knew what to do."

By the time Lacey left for the evening, Megan was up and around with no side effects from the bug at all. Her mind refused to stop, and she stayed up late watching old movies and eating the leftover cinnamon rolls, a whole plate of them.

The next two days, the same sickness came again. By the second evening, Megan called Dr. Stevens's office. He had received her medical files already, and she set an appointment for the next morning.

When she arrived, she was feeling just as bad as the previous days. She was late for the appointment since she couldn't tear herself from the bathroom.

Her hair was in tangles, her skin clammy, and she had bags under her eyes. One look at her and Dr. Stevens smiled.

"Well, my dear, I've been in this business for over sixty years, and I can tell you now, it's not the flu."

"It's not?" Megan asked, sitting on the examination table, moaning with the slight motion, which felt like a rocking boat to her.

"No, but let's run some tests before I go shooting off my old mouth." He grinned at her.

He drew blood, made her pee in a cup, and gave her a complete physical. Then he left the room for a few minutes and returned with an even bigger smile.

"Knew I wasn't wrong. I can spot it from a mile away," he mumbled, writing something in the folder.

"What?" Megan asked.

"Pregnancy." He smiled.

Megan's jaw hit the floor. "What is? Who is? What?" Megan stuttered.

"You, my dear, about seven and a half weeks, I would say, which would make it a February baby.

I'll need to know some more information to get an exact due date, but mid-February would be my first guess. Maybe even a Valentine's baby." He winked at her.

Megan had yet to breathe or blink. She stared at the old man like he was insane. He kept right on talking in a cheery voice while he wrote in the file.

"It's been a while since I brought a new life into Pride." He gazed off at the wall like he was trying to remember something important. "Not too many young couples settle down here. Oh boy! The joy of bringing a new life into this world!"

When these words hit Megan's brain, the realization finally hit her. "A baby!"

Chapter Fourteen

"A baby?" she asked again.

Dr. Stevens turned in his chair and looked at her.

"Are you saying that we, that I'm going to have a baby?" she asked again.

They'd been so careful. Seven and a half weeks meant their first time. But they had used protection that first night. Then she remembered that next morning when she'd woken him up, and the blood drained from her face.

An hour later, she was sitting at her kitchen table, looking at the pills Dr. Stevens had given her. Some were vitamins she would take every day, and others were to help with the morning sickness.

Boomer was trying desperately to get her attention by pacing at her feet, meowing loudly. She'd forgotten to feed him this morning. Getting up, she went and grabbed his bowl. Just then, the phone rang. Setting the empty bowl back down, she answered it.

"Hi, babe, do you miss me?" It was Todd. For the span of about ten seconds, Megan's brain refused to think. Todd. She hadn't once thought of what he would think. Should she tell him on the phone or wait until he came back in town? She guessed something this huge should be told face-to-face.

Biting her lip, she answered, "Yes, when are you coming home?"

"Tomorrow. Are you okay? Lacey said you had the flu."

"Not the flu, just…um, not feeling well. Will you be home for dinner tomorrow night?" she asked.

"Yeah, sure. I should be there about seven. Are you sure you're okay? You sound a little funny. Is that Boomer whining?" he asked.

Megan glanced down at the cat pawing her pants and crying. "Yeah, oh, I, um, forgot to feed him today." She moved over and filled his bowl with two huge scoops. Boomer gave her a look as if to say, "It's about time," and then went on happily eating. "I've been kind of busy."

"Lacey said you have your first customers coming tomorrow. Congratulations," he said happily.

"Oh yeah, I forgot. They're supposed to check in by noon. A family. They'll be spending three nights. I've also had other bookings too." She got a little excited thinking about it.

"That's wonderful. If you need any help…" He sounded excited, too.

"No, Lacey and Iian have been great with planning the meals. Hopefully, things will go smoothly." She chewed her lip.

"I think about you." The statement was simple, yet it caused Megan's heart to leap.

"Me too. I shouldn't miss you, but I do. I can't stop myself from thinking about you. I don't know what to do. I have a lot to think about after today… I have to ask myself what it is I want. I can tell you this—I know I've never felt this way before. It's almost like I've known you for a long time, like we're…" She hadn't wanted to say *connected*.

"Connected?" Todd said. "I feel it too. I know it's crummy timing, but I love you, Megan. I think I've always loved you. God, I wish I could tell you when you're in my arms so I could see your face."

Megan didn't know what to say. How could she be falling so fast for someone? What power did he hold over her? Whatever it was, it scared her. A silent tear fell on her hand, and she reached up to brush another off her cheek.

"You don't have to say anything now, only know that's how I feel. I would never do anything to hurt you."

"I know that. I trust you, but I have to trust myself," she whispered.

"Do your thinking tonight, Megan. I'll be there at seven tomorrow night. Good night. I love you," he said softly.

"Good night, Todd," she whispered back.

That night, Megan got about an hour of sleep. Boomer wasn't happy with her for the delay in the food, so he'd promptly gone to his pillow after dinner and didn't stir when she came upstairs several hours later.

The next morning, she felt the same: sick. She took her pills, and within the hour, it was manageable. She no longer felt a need to rush to the restroom. She still felt woozy, but not so bad. She could go along with her day.

The guests arrived early. They were a lovely family with two small boys who ran around in the grass while their parents happily chatted on the front porch.

Boomer let the two boys crawl all over him, then went and sat in the grass, flicking his tail and watching them play.

By early afternoon, the family headed out to sightsee and Megan was left to start dinner.

She decided to make a romantic dinner all by herself. She was going to tell Todd the news over dessert, and her nerves were high. She only knew how to make one meal: spaghetti.

When the noodles and meat sauces were simmering, she put the garlic bread in the oven. She set the nice dishes in the formal dining room, then quickly ran up, showered, and put on the new clothes she'd bought. It was a simple green skirt with a matching blouse. She knew it would only fit for another few months, but she didn't care since she looked good in it now.

It felt good to go shopping and pick out her own clothes. She remembered a fight she'd had with Derek over buying things. It was after she'd purchased a new pair of shoes one day. Her shoe had broken while she had been walking the two blocks to her office from the bus stop. She had to ride the bus, since he'd taken her car away from her. There was a small boutique next to her office building.

"Who the hell gave you the right to spend my hard-earned money on those ugly things?" Derek slammed his fist down on the kitchen table. The table was all set and looking just how he liked it with the silverware, plates, napkins, and glasses all in place. She'd purchased carryout at the Italian

restaurant on her bus ride home. The table was decorated and the food had been placed nicely on the dishes.

"I'm sorry; I broke my shoe walking to work. I couldn't go in wearing only one shoe." She prayed it would stop at that. She made sure to use the right tone of voice.

His dish flew through the air, right past her head. It hit the dining room wall, shattering with a loud crash, which made her jump.

"Damn it, Megan." He stood up. She didn't like it when he stood above her. "I work hard, and all I ask is for is a wife who obeys." He bent down, putting his face close to hers. She could feel his breath and see the red in his eyes. She knew this time it wasn't going to stop anytime soon.

"You spend all my money on those shoes. The least you can do is get a pair that isn't ugly as sin. I mean, look at them." He jerked her chair out from the table, pulling her along with it to expose the simple black pumps. She tried to sit as still as possible. His beefy hands rested on the arms of her chair. She was blocked in, nowhere to go.

"I'm sorry, Derek. I should have called you. I should have come home." She tried to make herself smaller, tried to hold her breath. She would have tried anything to prevent what was coming next.

The slap had come quickly; the stinging had lasted longer. She knew the fight wasn't over her shoes. She knew the slaps and hits weren't her fault. It was hard to think of anything other than surviving when a two-hundred-pound man was sitting on your chest, hitting you.

Clearing her head with a quick shake, she focused on the here and now. She thought about the future, her future and the baby's future.

She had at one point decided against children altogether, but that was when she was with Derek. She didn't want to raise children in a life like that, so she'd hidden the birth control patch from him. But a child with Todd…She could tell he would be a great father. But what would this do to her newfound freedom? She didn't believe in raising children in a single-parent home; she'd lived through that herself.

A brother for a mother and father. Not that Matt had done a bad job. It was just, as far back as she could remember, she'd wanted a woman to talk to, a mother figure. Sure, there were women Matt had dated, but he would never involve them in their life to the point where Megan felt comfortable around them.

When she was heading back down the stairs, the doorbell rang. Mentally calming herself, she pulled it open and was greeted by a bundle of white flowers. They covered Todd's face as he held them.

When he pulled them down so their eyes could connect, she noticed he too was dressed up. He wore black slacks and a blue shirt.

He looked very handsome, and it made Megan happy to see that he also wanted to have a special evening.

When Todd saw Megan, he instantly grew worried. Her face was paler than normal, and she had dark circles under her eyes. It looked like she'd dropped some weight.

But then he noticed the green number she wore. It was short and tight, showing off her long legs and every curve. Had her breasts gotten bigger, or was it some magic, feminine secret making them look that way? Either way, he enjoyed the view. Her hair was down, flowing around her shoulders in a wave. He smiled up at her.

"You're beautiful." He whispered it. He pulled her close and lightly kissed her lips, keeping it soft.

"You smell so good. God, I've missed you," he said, burying his face in her hair. She held on to him as if she didn't want to let go.

He could feel her body start to relax; she'd been very tense when he pulled her close. He ran his hand over her long hair and held her head to his shoulders. "What's wrong, baby?"

Then she started shaking, and whispered into his shoulder, "I'm pregnant. I wanted to tell you over dessert, but I just…"

Todd pulled back quickly, grabbed her shoulders, and looked into her teary eyes. He'd anticipated seeing the scared look in her eyes but hadn't expected to see a faint smile on her lips.

Todd let out a loud, "Whoop!" and spun her in a circle, then promptly picked her up and deposited her on the couch. Then the worry seeped in.

"Are you okay? I mean, we need to go see the doctor. I'll have to call Dr. Stevens…" He trailed off as he paced the floor in front of the couch. "Do you need to go to the hospital? You were sick." He started to pale. "Oh my God, you've been sick. We need to…"

Megan interrupted. "I've already seen Dr. Stevens. He says I'm about seven and a half weeks, and the baby is healthy. He gave me some vitamins and pills to help with the morning sickness."

Todd knelt before her. "Are you all right? It's not too bad?"

"I'm fine, only a little tired all the time. The pills help with the sickness." She placed her hand on his smooth face. "I don't want to worry you. I know what happened to Sara."

Todd pulled her close. “God, Megan, what happened with Sara and the baby isn’t going to happen now. It was a freak deal. She’d been sick beforehand. I know this wasn’t planned, but I pray you’re not sorry.”

“How can I be sorry? I know the timing is off, but no, I’m not sorry. I can’t help love what we’ve made.” She put a protective hand on her flat stomach. “It’s just, it kind of takes the decision out of my hands.”

“I know you wanted to take some time to start a new life, but can’t *we* be that new life?” he said, placing a hand over hers on her stomach and smiling up at her. “I have something else for you besides the flowers.” He was still kneeling before her when he pulled a small gray box from his coat pocket.

“Megan, I love you so much, I can’t imagine another day without you in my life. Please say you’ll marry me, start a new life with me and our baby.”

The ring was simply beautiful, a diamond on a titanium band.

“Todd, I can’t,” she whispered, holding up her hands. “I won’t marry someone out of necessity. I can’t lose myself again.”

"Megan, I'm nothing like your ex." Todd held the hurt and anger inside; he knew it wasn't what she needed now.

"Please." She pushed the ring back towards him. "Give me more time. I need to be okay with this first."

Just then, the kitchen fire alarm went off, causing them both to jump.

"Oh, my bread!" She raced into the kitchen. As he watched her back, he vowed that by the end of this year, he would change her mind. Maybe not tonight, but eventually. He knew it was the best for both of them, for all three of them.

The bread was a loss, but the spaghetti was perfect. Todd ate three helpings while keeping the conversation light and away from any talk of marriage.

Later, they sat on the front porch, giggling about Boomer, who was swatting fireflies. He'd gained so much weight, they were thinking of putting him on a diet.

Megan leaned back, placing her head on his shoulder and letting out a sigh. Summer was in full swing, and she loved how the evenings cooled off. Fall was around the corner and next year, they would have a baby.

Todd sat with Megan's head resting on his shoulder. He felt her entire body relax and knew she was tired. He rubbed her shoulder, and when he felt she was asleep, he gently carried her upstairs to bed. Her removed her clothing and then his and crawled in beside her to sleep.

The next morning, Megan rushed to the bathroom. She made sure to take the pill when her stomach would allow her to swallow some water. Half an hour later, she was feeling much better.

Todd stood outside the locked bathroom door, not knowing what to do. He paced back and forth, begging Megan to let him in so he could help. He knew there really wasn't anything he could do, except give comfort.

Once she emerged, he enveloped her in a long hug, murmuring sweet words in her hair. "Is it okay if I move my things over here today? I don't want to be apart from you, not for a moment," he said as they headed downstairs.

"That would be wonderful." Megan gave him a quick kiss and smile.

She knew either Lacey or Iian would be in the kitchen setting up breakfast for her guests. She couldn't wait to pass the news on.

She could hear the family who had rented the cabin eating in the formal dining room. The sounds of children drifted through the house, making it feel even more comfortable. When had she gotten used to people coming and going in her home? When had she started thinking of this as her home?

"Good morning," Megan said to the family. "How did you sleep?"

"Oh, wonderful. It's so quiet here. I think that's the first time in my life that I've woken to the birds singing," the woman, Stephanie, said, smiling at Todd over her coffee.

"This is Todd Jordan," Megan said. "Todd, this is Mr. and Mrs. Buckner, our guests, and their children, Brian and Bobby."

"How do you do? I hope you're enjoying your stay."

"Are you related to Lacey? She made the most wonderful breakfast," Mr. Buckner said, pointing to the pile of food on the table that their boys were inhaling.

"Yes, she's my sister. I'll go find her. Good day." He went back to the kitchen, leaving Megan to chat with the family.

When she went into the kitchen, Lacey had a fresh cup of coffee ready for her. Todd leaned against the counter with a smile on his face, his legs crossed at the ankle. He looked so comfortable in her kitchen, she knew he'd always belonged here.

Megan looked at the cup Lacey handed her. Setting it down on the counter, she said, "I better drink some juice instead this morning."

At Lacey's confused look, Megan glanced towards Todd for some help. Todd walked over and pulled Megan to his side.

"We're pregnant." He smiled at his sister.

"Whoo-hoo!" Lacey rushed over and hugged both of them, tears coming to her eyes. "I knew something was up. You're right, no coffee for the mother-to-be. I'm so happy. Wow! A baby!" she said, wiping the tears away.

This was the first time Megan had seen Lacey at a loss for words or, for that matter, surprised. Lacey always seemed to know what would happen before it did.

After breakfast, the family went on their way to go sightseeing. Lacey stayed and ate breakfast with them, then headed on her way to work.

Megan and Todd spent some time sitting on the front porch, talking. The cabins were booked almost through the end of summer, and she was getting Internet reservations for the fall and as late as Christmas.

"It appears you have yourself a successful business. I hope you haven't taken on too many responsibilities with the baby coming."

Megan hadn't thought of it that way. "I talked to a young woman at the store the other day, Nancy something. She said she'd been looking for work. Maybe I can hire her part-time," Megan said, chewing her lip.

"Nancy Webber. She is Iian's age. She has a couple of kids, I think. She would be perfect."

"I'll call her today and see about setting up a schedule."

With that settled, Todd headed into his office. Since he'd been out of town for the last week, he needed to catch up on some paperwork. Megan had things that needed to be done before lunchtime when her new guests were due to arrive.

She busied herself with inside chores, cleaning the cabin and making sure everything in the other cabin was ready for the new guests.

The young couple arrived right before Iian, who brought some turkey and roast beef sandwiches for the guests. They set the lunches out on the porch table for guests to help themselves.

Everyone enjoyed eating out on the porch, chatting about a visit to the beach and how to get to the national park. The young couple was heading into town for some shopping before they headed out to sightsee. Megan made a point to mention Allison's store. The couple seemed eager to stop there for some pictures and knickknacks.

After Iian and the guests left to go about their afternoon, Megan decided to spend some time outside. It was too nice a day to go back inside. She spent time in her small garden area out back, where she'd planted some vegetables.

Boomer rolled around in the fresh dirt. He swatted at flies that buzzed by or glared at birds as they drifted overhead.

She was digging up some fresh carrots when Boomer let out a loud hiss and ran off towards the garage. Megan glanced up and watched his tail disappear inside the doors. Then a shadow fell over her. Without looking, she knew who it was. Her happy new world disappeared.

Chapter Fifteen

Todd was drowning in paperwork. He enjoyed a good, healthy stack of work now and then, but this was ridiculous. His desk looked like he'd been out of town for a month instead of only one week.

Iian had stopped by earlier and had brought him a sandwich for lunch. He'd heard the happy news from Lacey and had come over to congratulate him.

He told him of the new couple that had checked in before lunch. He'd given Todd an update on Megan, saying she looked tired, but she'd eaten a good lunch before he left her.

After Iian's visit, Todd started back on the stack of papers. He wanted to finish up early so he could get back home. He liked the picture his mind drew when he thought of that word: Megan sitting on the front porch waiting for him with Boomer lying on her lap. He could imagine kids running around the front yard, a boy and a girl who had Megan's eyes. His daydream was broken by the sound of his phone ringing.

"Jordan Shipping," he answered.

"Todd Jordan?" came a deep voice. The connection was bad, and he could barely hear.

"This is Todd. May I help you?"

"Todd, this is Mark. I have some news about Megan Kimble's ex-husband. He escaped yesterday morning. Apparently, they were moving him to a minimum-security prison when he overpowered a guard. He shot and killed the man. He's been missing since then."

Todd slammed down the phone and then quickly picked it up again and called the house. After the fifth ring, he slammed it down again. Calling the police on his cell phone, he rushed out the door.

He knew Megan didn't like that he was watching out for her, but she was part of his life now.

Apparently, Derek had used the guard's ID to jump a small plane from Boston and had landed in Portland this morning. Using the man's credit card, he'd rented a white sedan. Relaying this information to the police over the phone, Todd prayed he wasn't too late. Megan could just be in the yard or visiting with the new boarders.

When he arrived at the house less than five minutes later, the sheriff was already there. Sheriff Robert Brogan, who had been a high school friend of his, had his hand on his gun as he came around from the side yard.

When he saw it was Todd, he moved his hand away from his gun.

Todd jumped from the car after it came to a stop beside the Jeep.

"Megan, Megan," he screamed, running up the front stairs. He bolted across the porch and threw open the front door.

Robert came up beside him. "She's not here. I arrived about two minutes ago. No sign of a struggle in the house. I checked out back in the garage and found a cat out there, but it wouldn't let me get near it. The front door was left wide open. Could she have gone up to one of the cabins?"

"You take the farthest ones and I'll check the closer ones." As they sprinted off, Todd's mind ran through the conversations they'd had about her ex and what he'd done to her. He searched his memory for any information that might help him locate her.

He remembered the story she'd told him of Derek locking her away for weeks at a time. He prayed the bastard didn't have his hands on her.

He prayed she was alive. *Just let her be alive.*

Megan opened her eyes a little. Her tongue felt thick and dry. Her head throbbed, and her eyes could barely focus. She could only see shapes and colors.

She was lying on a bed, and her hands were tied behind her. There was a rag in her mouth, stuffed so far in that it almost caused her to gag.

The back of her head hurt; something sticky slid down her neck. Her legs were either tied or being held down. She tried to move and realized Derek was in the process of tying them. Immediately, she started kicking until she felt her knee connect with something solid and she heard a grunt.

"Stupid bitch, hold still." She kicked and struggled harder. When she thought he had her pinned down, her foot connected with something solid again, and he went down, falling backward off the bed.

She could hear him cussing, but she didn't stop to think. Instead, she jumped up from the bed and ran over to kick him some more. Because her hands were tied behind her, she couldn't open the door without him getting to her first.

She plowed her foot into the side of his head. This time he stayed down, his eyes closed. Blood poured from a cut on his lip and one above his eye.

Jumping over him, she ran to the door and turned backward to use her tied hands to open it. It took her a minute to turn the handle. As she turned to run out, she was thrown clear of the door, back across the bed. She bounced off the mattress, hitting the floor hard and landing on her hip.

The wind was knocked from her lungs, but the single piece of duct tape Derek had used snapped free. Pushing herself up, she saw him lock the door with a jerk.

"You stupid bitch! I'll teach you." She could see the rage on his face as it turned redder. He had changed a lot in the last couple of months. The first time he was in jail, he had gained ten pounds. Now, however, he'd lost a lot of it and was also almost completely bald. The remaining hair was cut very short. His eyes darted around the room as if he was high. His blue shirt and pants were too small for him, and his gut showed under the shirt. "They let me go. I walked right out of there. They said I had to teach you how to be a good wife." His lip was bleeding and his right eye was starting to close shut. She had to get out of this room. Her life and the baby's life depended on it.

Looking around, she noticed a window beside the door. Thick drapes hung over it, closing out the light and the world. She had to get to the door or that window.

Megan yanked down her gag and tossed it across the room at him. "I'm not your wife! They didn't let you go!"

"Shut up! You don't know anything! You're a stupid slut. You belong to me. I have to teach you. You think you can live after what you did to me?" He started walking again

"Derek, you have to let me go. Don't come near me. Don't ever lay a hand on me again!" she yelled. Scooting away, she stood up and backed towards the wall.

"Oh, big words. You can't hurt me!" he screamed, and pulled a gun from his back pocket. He waved it around. "You'll know I'm in charge. I have always been in charge, and you're a stupid slut who couldn't keep her damn legs closed. You think I didn't know about all the men you fucked? You're nothing but a whore. You deserve to be treated like a whore. I've been thinking about this for months, what I'd do when I got my hands on you. Well, I can tell you, you're going to enjoy me, honey." He moved towards her again, his free hand on his belt.

Megan saw the gun waver between her head and her heart. She put a hand over her stomach and knew it was over.

Todd raced towards the house. He and Robert had checked all the cabins, but Megan was nowhere to be found. "We've put an APB out on the sedan he rented. How did you get that information anyway?" Robert asked when they reached the main house.

"I had a PI watching this guy. I'm going to drive around and see if I can find her," he said, heading towards the Jeep.

"Todd, let the police handle this. We'll find her," he said.

"No! I will! And when I find him, I'm—"

"Don't!" Robert broke in. "You stay out of this Todd, you hear? I've got my deputies driving around looking for the car."

"Damn it, they could be halfway across Oregon by now." Todd jumped in the Jeep and pulled out, crossing the yard. He drove through town, going about sixty. He imagined Derek would stop somewhere; he just didn't know where. He thought of heading back up towards Portland, but instead of turning left, he headed right. Edgeview was only ten minutes away, and on instinct, he headed there. He called the house and told Lacey what was going on. Both she and Iian were going to start searching.

"Don't worry, Todd, we'll find her," Lacey said. Todd could hear Iian in the background and knew they would help.

When he reached Edgeview five minutes later, he started looking for the sedan. He was passing by the outskirts of town when he spotted the car parked on the side of a small out-of-the-way motel.

Phoning Robert, he told him he'd check it out. Robert told him to stay put, not to do anything, that he would contact the Edgeview police. He could be there in fifteen minutes. Fifteen minutes could mean the difference between life and death. Todd parked the Jeep and got out.

Derek stalked towards her. He undid his belt and struggled with his zipper. The only light came from the bedside lamp and she could see he was hard against the jeans he was trying to unzip. The thought of this man touching her made her stomach spin.

He started waving the gun again. "Now you be a good wife and lay down on the bed and spread your legs for your husband. It shouldn't be too hard for a slut like you," he said, reaching for her.

She only had one chance to survive. Without another glance at the gun, she pushed away from the wall.

As Todd reached for the door handle to the front office, he heard a loud crash. He saw movement to his right, three windows down. Lying on the cement was a small body tangled in thick drapes.

The door to the room flew open, and a short, thick, bald man ran out, waving a gun. Without a thought for his own safety, Todd ran towards the man.

"You stupid bitch!" The man pointed the gun and drew back his foot to kick the mound lying on the cement.

"No! Megan!" Todd yelled.

Derek's head and the gun snapped up. Megan threw off the curtains and kicked the man in the shins with all her weight. Derek went down hard on his knees, the gun wavering in his hand, and then Todd was on him.

She'd been almost in a dream state before jumping out the window, knowing the only hope of survival for her and the baby was to get out of that room. She'd prayed the room was on the ground floor.

As she lay on the hard cement, encased in the thick drapes, trying to catch her breath, she heard Todd yell her name and watched as Derek swung the gun towards him.

All thoughts left her. All she could imagine was life without Todd. There would be no life for her without him.

She saw murder in Todd's eyes. It wasn't aimed at her, never aimed at her, only to protect her. In that instant, she realized she loved him. Beyond anything she'd ever felt for anyone else in her entire life, she loved Todd.

Derek's legs were right next to her feet. Kicking as hard as she could, she hit him in the shins, and he fell down almost on top of her.

Then Todd got Derek in a headlock and pounded his fist into his face. The gun flew out of Derek's hand and landed on the cement with a dull thud.

Several people poked their heads out their doors after hearing the commotion, and they gathered around to stare at the scene.

"Call the police!" Megan screamed at a middle-aged woman who stood there in complete shock.

"Todd, stop!" Todd was pounding his fist so fast and hard, Derek was now unconscious, slumped against the wall. Megan could see that his eyes were swollen shut, his mouth was bleeding, and his nose appeared broken. She jumped up from the ground, her hip screaming at her, and ran over to Todd.

Todd was focused on each blow, but she had to get him to stop. “Todd! Stop, I’m okay, please, Todd. Stop!” She grabbed his fist as he threw another punch. He looked up from the slumped figure and looked deep in her eyes. He took a breath and shook his head clear.

“I’m okay. We’re okay.” She wrapped her arms around him.

Chapter Sixteen

"Oh, God! Megan?" He picked her up, holding her close. Blood ran down the side of her head, and she had cuts and pieces of glass in her arms. He shook uncontrollably. He walked several paces and glanced back over his shoulder at two large men who stood over Derek. "Make sure he stays put until the cops get here."

"This man isn't going anywhere," the larger of the two men said, rolling Derek to his back. "You got him real good."

"I called the police," the middle-aged woman said, coming out the office door. "Are you all right, honey?" she asked Megan.

"I'm fine," Megan said as Todd carried her towards the Jeep. "Todd, where are we going?"

"Hospital," he said and set her gently in the Jeep. "Damn cops and ambulances take too long." He put her seat belt around her. "Tell them if they want my statement, I'll be at the hospital," he said to the woman, who nodded in reply.

Several hours later, after being checked into the hospital and having doctors look at her, Megan lay back on a soft bed, resting in a private room.

The baby was all right.

She kept saying it over and over. They'd listened to the heartbeat, and it was nice and strong. Todd cried when he heard it. Megan was so touched by his tears that she broke down too.

She had a couple of stitches in her shoulder and head. The doctor removed lots of glass from her back and arms, but for the most part, the thick curtains had shielded her. Her hip was badly bruised and her ankle twisted, but other than that, she felt fine. She felt free.

Todd paced up and down the room, mumbling about something, while the nurse took Megan's blood pressure.

"The doctor wants you to take a sleeping pill to relax. He would like to keep you overnight."

"Oh no, I think I'd like to go ho—" she started.

"We'll stay," Todd broke in, nodding at the nurse.

Megan glanced at his face and saw his concern. "Thank you," she said to the nurse, smiling, as she gave her the pill and some water.

There was a knock at the door. "Miss Kimble?" A tall young man in a sheriff's uniform stood right inside the door. "I'm Sheriff Brogan. The doctor says it's all right to talk to you. Do you have a few minutes?"

"Come on in, Robert," Todd said from the corner.

"Oh, Todd, didn't see you there. I'd like a couple of minutes with you too." He nodded.

The nurse quietly went out after making sure Megan swallowed the small pill.

Todd walked over and sat next to Megan, pulling her bandaged hand into his own.

"I have a few questions about what happened. Do you feel up to answering them? It won't take long."

"She just took a sleeping pill," Todd started in.

"I feel fine. Go ahead." Megan squeezed his hand.

Ten minutes later, after answering a dozen or so questions, Megan felt very sleepy. Todd was telling Robert his side of the story, and she drifted off listening to his soothing voice.

Todd could feel Megan's hand grow lax in his as he finished telling what had happened at the motel.

Robert finished taking notes. "Well, it's a federal matter now since the officer he killed was a federal guard. He's going to be put away for a long time."

"That's good," Todd murmured, looking down at Megan. She was pale and her hair was pushed back from her face. White bandages covered her arms and shoulder. Then he looked down at the bandages on his own fists. Megan had been so concerned when she'd seen that some of the blood on his hands was his own, she'd gone white and demanded that he be fixed up as well.

"You did a fine job on that guy. Knocked a couple of teeth out and broke his nose. He's in the hospital ward at the state facility. He'll be there another few days, and then they'll ship him back East." Robert sat with Todd for another few minutes until Iian and Lacey walked in, both carrying vases of flowers.

"She's asleep," Todd whispered and signed. He ushered them both in.

"How is she?" Lacey asked, moving over to Megan and looking down at her. She was pale and had a few cuts on her hands, but she looked well and alive. "How's the baby?"

"They're both fine." He moved over and kissed his sister's cheek. "The baby is fine. We heard the heartbeat," he said with a proud grin.

Iian signed his questions, and Todd answered, telling them both a shorter version of the story. By the time he was done telling his story, he was exhausted.

"Why don't you lie down for a while? I can watch over her," Lacey said, nodding towards the pull-out bed. Instead, Todd pulled his shoes off and scooted Megan over so that her head rested on his shoulder. She didn't even stir. Lacey covered them both with a blanket. When Iian signed to her that they should leave, she turned down the lights and headed out with her brother.

Dr. Stevens walked into Megan's hospital room the next morning followed by a tall blond man wearing a white medical jacket and with a stethoscope casually wrapped around his neck. When he glanced up from the chart, he gave Megan a quick smile, showing off a perfect set of the whitest teeth she'd ever seen.

"Megan, how are you feeling?" Dr. Stevens asked, taking Megan's attention off the blond gentlemen. "I heard we had quite an exciting day yesterday."

"Yes. I'm fine…" she began, but he shushed her while he listened to her heart with a stethoscope.

When he was done, he said with a grin, "This is my grandson, Doctor Aaron Stevens. He's going to be helping me out for a while." The older Dr. Stevens moved over and started poking at Todd's hands while Dr. Aaron Stevens lightly shook Megan's bandaged hand.

"It's a pleasure, Miss Kimble," the younger man said. "I hear from my grandfather that we'll be neighbors. I've purchased the Bell place down the road."

Megan had yet to see the house, but she'd heard it was an old ranch house that needed a lot of work. "Oh, congratulations. Please call me Megan."

"Please call me Aaron," he said.

"I hadn't heard the Bells had moved," Todd interrupted, causing the young doctor to glance over at him for the first time.

"They decided to downsize since their children are all grown and married. They didn't want to maintain such a big place."

"Oh, are you married then?" Todd asked a little too eagerly.

"No." He turned back to Megan. "The place needs a lot of work. The Bells had let it go the last couple of years. It's kind of a project for me."

Todd let out a small grunt of disapproval. The young doctor started looking over Megan's bandages.

"We'd like to do an ultrasound. There's nothing to worry about. Everything looks fine, the baby's heartbeat is strong, but just to be on the safe side," Aaron said, continuing his exam of her arm and hand. Then he looked at the back of Megan's head. She had a small bandage over the two stitches she had received. "You had a nasty bump here. Are you feeling dizzy or nauseous? Other than the morning sickness?"

"No. They gave me my medicine early enough this morning that I feel fine."

"Good. Your stitches are clean; you should keep them dry for a few days." He looked down at her shoulder, where she had five more stitches. As he pulled her hospital gown down, Megan looked over at Todd. She could see concern and something else in his eyes. Protection.

The older Dr. Stevens pulled Todd's attention away, asking him to move his fingers. "Gave the man a good whooping, huh?" He chuckled. "From the sounds of it, he had it coming."

"Yes, sir." Todd pulled his gaze back from the old man to focus on the younger one, who was still checking out Megan's shoulder.

Megan could hear him mumbling under his breath.

"My grandson is going to be taking over for me when I retire next month." At this, Todd's eyes went back to the old man.

"What? You can't retire! I mean, who's going to deliver our baby?" He knew he sounded childish, but he didn't care.

Dr. Stevens saw the look and gripped Todd's hands harder, causing Todd to wince. The old man might be about a hundred years old, but his grip was that of a thirty-year-old.

"My grandson has been practicing medicine for eight years in California. Don't worry, my boy. I'll still be around town, just doing a lot more fishing and golfing." He smiled over at Megan and winked as he patted Todd's arm.

"Well, now," Aaron said, straightening back up and replacing Megan's gown over her bandaged shoulder. "It shouldn't take too long for the ultrasound." He moved to the door and pulled in a machine on wheels.

Todd walked over and stood next to Megan. "We'd like to be the first to welcome you to Pride."

Aaron looked between the two of them and smiled. "Thank you. Would you like to see your baby?"

Todd's face turned a little white, then his chest puffed out, and the silliest smile crossed his face.

Megan had wanted some privacy with Todd so she could tell him how she felt, but there was a blur of visitors after the doctors left. She liked both of them, the old and the young, especially after the younger made a point to go out of his way for Todd. He printed out pictures of the baby, which looked like nothing more than a small blob to her. She really liked him because he had signed her release papers. She could also tell Todd had warmed up to him.

Their drive home was pleasant, but again, they weren't alone. Lacey and Iian had arrived and insisted on driving them home. Lacey didn't want Todd to drive with his hands bandaged up, and Megan wasn't allowed to drive yet. Iian drove the Jeep home, and he reached the house a good five minutes before them.

In her absence, Lacey had seen to breakfast and lunch for her customers. She'd also cleaned both cabins and the main house. When they drove up in Lacey's oversize sedan, a whole group of townspeople stood on the porch, their hands full of dishes. It was going to be a long night.

Megan was propped up on the living room couch. Boomer made a point of complaining about her not being home last night and then snuggled up in her lap and continued purring.

Now, as the evening drew to an end, her energy drained away. Faces blurred together. When her head almost rolled off her shoulders, Lacey ushered everyone out of the house.

Todd walked over and picked her up in his arms. “Let me take you upstairs.”

“I’m just a little tired,” she said into his shoulder. He was making a habit of carrying her around, and she liked it.

“Good night,” Todd said to Lacey.

Lacey already had a handful of dishes. “I’ll clean up and lock up. Good night.”

After Todd laid Megan gently down on the bed, he pulled off her shoes and sat next to her.

“You gave me a scare,” he said, gently pushing her blonde hair behind her ear. “Don’t do it again.” He leaned down and placed a light kiss on the tip of her nose.

“I won’t as long as you don’t either. When I saw him point the gun at you…”

“Don’t.” He pulled her in for a hug. “Let’s not talk about it now.”

"I couldn't stand life without you. You know, I—I—," she stuttered against his shoulder. Pulling back from him, she looked him in the eyes. She wanted to see his face. "I love you. I think I've loved you from the first moment I laid eyes on you. You're my future. You're everything to me. I love you *so* much. Marry me, Todd."

Tears sprang to his eyes at the same time that a huge smile crossed his lips. Then he kissed her, and she knew she'd found what she'd always been looking for.

Epilogue

Megan's stomach was full of butterflies, and it had nothing to do with her morning sickness, which had ended last month. She stood in front of the mirror. She could just make out a small bump, which caused her to smile.

The short sleeves of the loose, flowing dress showed off her shoulders. Her scratches and bruises were gone and her skin looked smooth and pale. The dress's light cream color accented her complexion perfectly. Her hair was down, curling in small ringlets with flowers pinned in it. She glanced at her face in the reflection and enjoyed the glow in her eyes.

A soft knock sounded at the door, and she didn't even jump. "Come in," she said without taking her gaze from the mirror.

"Oh, you look wonderful," Lacey said, crossing the room and smiling at her. "It's time."

Megan blinked and turned around. Lacey handed her a small bouquet of pink roses and quickly hugged her.

As Megan walked down the stairs towards her backyard, which had been transformed for the wedding, she knew she'd feel just like this for the rest of her life. Happy.

If you've enjoyed this book, please consider leaving a review where you purchased it. Thanks! —Jill

Want a FREE copy of my Pride Series novella, Serving Pride? **Join my newsletter** at jillsanders.com *and get your copy today. You'll also* be *the first to hear about new releases, freebies, giveaways, and more.*

Follow Jill online at:

Web: www.jillsanders.com
Twitter: @jilllmsanders
Facebook: JillSandersBooks
Email: jill@jillsanders.com

Discovering Pride Preview

Chapter One

A cool breeze drifted over the tall trees, floating down towards the still waters of a large pond and causing the lily pads to stir. Dragonflies buzzed from flower to flower, and frogs hopped along the grassy shore.

Every now and then, a lone leaf would break free from a branch and float slowly down to the moss-covered forest floor. Soon it would be winter and this little piece of heaven would be covered in snow. All the insects and animals would be tucked away for the cold days and nights. But today the pond waters were buzzing with life.

Lacey Jordan was a free-spirited woman who enjoyed the fresh air, blue skies, and nature sounds that surrounded her home in Pride, Oregon. Even though summer was ending, the fall temperatures had reached a record high. A true Indian summer was in full swing.

Lacey was happily floating alone in the pond that bordered her property. Well, she wasn't quite alone;

Bernard had been running in and out of the water, digging in the mud near the shore. Bernard was Lacey's first love, and to date, her only. He was everything she wanted in a man: loyal, loving, brave, and a great listener. Not to mention he was blond, brown eyed, and loved to snuggle. His only faults were that he hogged the bed, slobbered a lot, and was extremely hairy, but no one was perfect.

Bernard was Lacey's three-and-a-half-year-old Labrador retriever.

As she floated in the water, her short black hair bobbed around her face, a face often described as pixie-like. Her straight nose was, in her opinion, her best asset, but most people claimed it was her crystal slate eyes that stood out the most. An artist who had once painted her compared her to an exotic creature from beyond this world.

A small crease formed between her eyebrows at the thought of being compared to an exotic or even mythical creature. It happened often and she was getting tired of it. To her, she was just Lacey, a down-to-earth woman in her mid-twenties whom, at this point, had yet to fall in love.

Most people in her town knew she had an uncanny way of predicting what was going to happen. Sometimes it seemed like she could even control the outcome. However, she knew that she just paid attention to everything more than other people did.

Today she didn't want to think of the town or its inhabitants. She forced herself to relax again as she studied the bright clear sky through the blanket of leaves on the trees overhead. Today she was going to enjoy her favorite place, the pond, which was in the woods between her house and her brother Todd's house.

Every once in a while Bernard would swim out to check on her or bark to make sure his presence was still known. She could spend hours out here, lost in thought, which would sometimes make her late for work. She was grateful she wasn't expected anywhere today so she could continue floating and relaxing as she pleased.

Lacey had been born and raised in Pride, and this was home. There had been a time when she'd craved travel, wanting to expand her horizons and become a woman of the world. However, after spending over a year traveling around Europe, she had needed to be home again. She had missed taking walks along the beach or sitting in front of a fire with her father and brothers. She had made it home only to lose her father and she had struggled through her loss. Her family needed her close and she needed them in return.

She started treading water as she remembered the weeks after she had come home. It had been a difficult time for the Jordan family, adjusting to the changes after the accident that had claimed their father's life and left their brother Iian battered and without his hearing. But the family had conquered a lot together, learning sign language and running the family businesses. They had learned to take care of each other.

Looking up, she saw Bernard happily running around the shore, chasing the ducks that kept trying to land.

Aaron Stevens was restless, hot, and sweaty. And he was horny. His *need* reminded him it had been over seven months since his breakup with Jennifer. He'd spent the last few days hammering away on his house, spending all his pent-up anger and hurt on demolition. Now, however, he was still hot, angry, sweaty, and horny.

When he had purchased the old house, he'd known it needed a lot of work. But he'd thought the project would help him keep his mind off the fact that he'd almost made the biggest mistake of his life. He had learned a valuable lesson in love, and it had only cost him his heart.

When he hit his thumb for the tenth time in the last half hour, he threw the hammer across the room. But because there were no walls in the place, it hit the floor with a dull thud, giving him no satisfaction.

The first thing he'd done was rip up the bright orange carpet, and now the entire house echoed. He had plans for hardwood or tile in the house, but he had yet to decide on which. All he knew was that the carpet had to go.

He stalked from the room, fuming and frustrated, his thumb throbbing like a bitch. When he reached the back door, he kept on going.

Soon he found himself on a path in a part of the woods he hadn't explored yet. There was a fork in the path, one that led to his closest neighbors, Megan and Todd Jordan. They had been his first patients after taking over his grandfather's medical practice.

He paused by the head of the path and remembered walking into the hospital room after Megan had been rescued from her crazy ex-husband.

Megan had seemed so small and pale, bruised by the whole ordeal, but she and Todd's unborn child had survived. Her ex-husband, Derek, was now on trial for the murder of a federal guard. Todd had hovered over her and protected her, which gained him instant respect in Aaron's book.

Aaron had done an ultrasound at the hospital, printing as many pictures as Todd had wanted. He felt compassion for the new family. They'd had a rough start, but he knew they would turn out okay.

The pregnant mother had been fine, and he had seen them again just yesterday for another checkup.

Aaron was almost to a clearing before he heard the dog barking. He was so deep in his thoughts, he hadn't realized how far and in which direction his wandering had taken him. Was he still on his property?

Just then, a wet yellow lab came running down the path towards him. The dog wagged its tail. Aaron held out his hand for it to smell as it ran up. The dog sniffed his hand and then licked it, wagging its tail at full speed the whole time. Then it quickly turned and ran off in the opposite direction.

Smiling after the animal, Aaron continued down the path. He came to a clearing with a good-sized pond in the middle of tall grass. The water looked calm and cool, so he decided to cool off before heading back to the house.

Tossing off his clothing quickly, he dove from a huge flat rock that hung over the water's edge. Cutting deep through the cool crisp water, he was halfway across the small pond when his body hit something solid—solid, but definitely soft. He reached up and getting a hand full of soft skin, pushed up from the muddy bottom.

Lacey heard Bernard run off down the path, barking. Thinking he was probably chasing a bird, she dove under the water one last time. She wanted to stop by Megan's later to see how she and the baby were doing. Maybe she would even make them dinner.

When she was in the middle of the pond, she bumped into something solid. Then she was grabbed and pulled upwards by warm hands.

"What do you think you're doing?" she sputtered after surfacing, shaking her head to clear it.

"Take your filthy hands off me." Lacey pushed against his chest, but he didn't budge. Shaking the water from her eyes, she got her first look at him.

Lacey felt his muscular, hairy legs against hers and she could see a light coat of blond hair on his tan chest. A chest, she noted, which was full of toned rippling muscles.

He looked like a Greek god. His hair was a mass of dripping, golden blond locks that were a little longer than her own. His skin was golden, his eyes were a deep rich brown, and he had a strong firm chin. His body was tight against her own and it was warm, firm, and naked. She pushed harder against his chest, but again he didn't budge.

His hands were holding the struggling creature and she was soft, small, and naked. Her hair was short, silky black, and it was slicked back from her face—a beautiful face at that. Her eyes were silver and seemed to penetrate into him, and she had a cute little nose that sloped up at the end. There was a very small dimple in her chin, and her lips were full and puckered ever so slightly. She had a look on her face that told him this was her pond and he was the intruder here.

"What do we have here?" Aaron said holding the squirming woman. She looked like a drenched pixie as he smiled down at her.

"Hmm, I don't think that my hands are dirty any longer," he said with a slow smile. He kicked his legs a few times, making sure their heads stayed above the water. He felt her legs against his; they were soft and smooth, making him want to tangle in them. He could see her chest rising and falling with each breath she took. The water lapped lower on the most perfect pair of breast he'd ever had the pleasure of seeing in his almost thirty years. She tried to push him away again, but he pulled her closer until he could feel her cool skin against his burning skin.

"Let's see what happens when I…" He lowered his head, intent on tasting.

When his head started descending towards her mouth, she whispered in a shaky voice, "Let me go before I scream."

He heard the panic in her voice. Pulling his head away, he looked into her eyes and he could see the panic there.

Shaking his head to clear it, he pulled away from her just as she reached up and pushed his head under the water. He stayed under for a moment, allowing his mind to cool.

In that moment, he saw her duck under the water. She quickly ran her eyes over him, turned her back, and swam towards the shore at a speed that impressed him.

He drifted under the water for another few seconds, trying to clear his head. When he pushed himself up, he shook the water from his eyes and looked towards the shore. He didn't see anyone. Where had she disappeared to? He glanced around, but she was nowhere to be found. How could she have disappeared so quickly? There were some bushes and a rock to the left, but nothing big enough to conceal a woman. Turning in circles, he scanned the entire area, looking for any movement. Nothing!

Was he going crazy? What was he doing? Had she even really existed? Had he imagined her? No!

He could still feel the warmth from her breath on his face, and when he closed his eyes, he could smell her. Dunking his head under the water again, he looked around the pond. From what he could see, he was the only inhabitant. Pushing up again, he scanned one more time and then finally called out.

"Hello?" Nothing!

He must have been hornier then he'd thought to imagine a sexy water pixie. Shaking his head, he decided he could use a few laps to cool his libido.

Other titles by Jill Sanders

The Pride Series

Finding Pride – Pride Series #1

Discovering Pride – Pride Series #2

Returning Pride – Pride Series #3

Lasting Pride – Pride Series #4

Serving Pride – Prequel to Pride Series #5

Red Hot Christmas – A Pride Christmas #6

My Sweet Valentine – Pride Series #7

The Secret Series

Secret Seduction – Secret Series #1

Secret Pleasure – Secret Series #2

Secret Guardian – Secret Series #3

Secret Passions – Secret Series #4

Secret Identity – Secret Series #5

Secret Sauce – Secret Series #6

The West Series

Loving Lauren – West Series #1

Taming Alex – West Series #2

Holding Haley – West Series #3

Missy's Moment – West Series #4

Breaking Travis - West Series #5

Roping Ryan - West Series #6

FINDING PRIDE

ISBN: 978-1480054547

Copyedited by Erica Ellis – www.inkdeepediting.com

About the Author

Jill Sanders is the New York Times and USA Today bestselling author of the Pride Series, the Secret Series, and the West Series romance novels. Having sold over 150,000 books within six months of her first release, she continues to lure new readers with her sweet and sexy stories. Her books are available in every English-speaking country, available in audio books, and are now being translated into six different languages.

Born as an identical twin in a large family, she was raised in the Pacific Northwest. She later relocated to Colorado for college and a successful IT career before discovering her talent as a writer. She now makes her home in charming rural Florida where she enjoys the beach, swimming, hiking, wine tasting, and, of course, writing.